COLD WORLD

by

CARDE'L

Book design by Final Draft Design
Book editing by Tiffany Horn

Published by Richard Jenkins for BLOCK STAR BOOKS

Printed in the United States of America

Carde'l contact info: *cardelunlimited@gmail.com*
Instagram: @CARD_E_L
Twitter: @CardelWrites

First and foremost I want to give all praise and glory to MY CREATOR. It is only through His grace that I am still here.

To my beautiful princess Za-Za, my time away from you is almost over and I'll be home real soon. The thought of you gives me the strength and determination I need to keep moving.

Dee Dee, my niece, I am very proud of you and all of your academic accomplishments. Keep moving forward! To my nephew Poppie, I'll be your number one fan when you make it to the NFL. To my other nieces and nephews, never stop reaching for the stars! I love you.

To my sister Nakia, my mother Angela, my father Richard, my sisters Ashley and Quinetta, Aunt Tasha, and Uncle Larry, I don't know how I would have overcome the many obstacles that life has thrown my way without your unconditional love and steadfast support. Words can't express how truly grateful I am to have you in my life.

To my Aunt Dinka, Aunt Nicky, my, Shaniqua, Valencia, and to the rest of my family…I love y'all.

Harlem, thank you for being there. SHOUT OUT TO Cheese, Tat, Barlow, Tutt, Tiffany, New Money, Odrama, Weeze, Tyon, Mike, Chinese, Judy, Suge, Nesha, and Tiff. Shout out to the entire Dolly Holmes Projects, MLK Boulevard, and Wilber Section. Big ups to Trenton!!!! Too many names to remember…It's all love.

I would also like to give a shout out to my close friend, Tiffany Horn. You played a very important role in helping me get this project off the ground, and I appreciate all your help.

R.I.P Turk (My brother Rich), M.H., Break Bread, Rob, Paulie, and Looch.

Free Joseph Townsend, Paper Boy, Paylay, Taz, and Tyson.

CHAPTER 1: MOTHER AND SON

It was a hot summer night in Trenton, New Jersey. The only thing that gave light to the extremely dark alley way was the bright stars that shone down from the pitch black sky, and the dim light from the tall street lamp at the far end of the corner. The alley was cluttered with wooden boards, bricks, and broken glass that was scattered all over the ground. Gusto turned into the alley way, looking back at his mother who walked several steps behind him. "Come on mom, hurry up!", Gusto was frustrated with his mother's slow pace. The huge rose gold Jesus medallion that hung from his rose gold chain swayed from side to side as he carefully tried not to trip over the debris on the ground. Gusto was mixed with Jamaican descent and was a slick talking, witty, overly courageous street hustler that stood 6 feet tall with a husky frame. His light brown skin, light brown eyes, and full pink lips caused everyone he came across to think he was a pretty boy. That was until they saw the permanent scar stretching from his neck to his ear, and the chipped tooth in the front of his mouth. These battle wounds solidified Gusto's ruff neck status, just like a lot of other people growing up in the hood.

"Damn boy calm down, here I come", his mother stated while sucking her teeth. Alley Cat was her name, and doing whatever it took to smoke crack was her game. She was a slim built light skin woman that was about five foot four inches tall. She was only 38 years old, but the several years she spent running the streets getting high aged her dramatically. Her afro-like hair was nappy and matted down. She had a lazy left eye, and her oversized lips were always crusty, and she only had six dirty teeth left in her mouth. "Stand right there and look out", Gusto demanded before climbing through a small opening in a fence. He landed in a junky backyard of an abandoned building. Gusto bent down to move aside a long wooden board that lay on the ground, and then grabbed a small clear plastic bag of crack. Hustling out of the junky alley way was beneficial to Gusto because it made it extremely difficult for the police to find his stash whenever they ran down.

Gusto quickly cut back through the fence. "Hurry up and come on." Alley Cat stepped towards her son, who was breaking off a piece of crack from his boulder. Gusto dropped the piece in to her dirty hand. That's when Alley Cat began to examine it's size and sucked her teeth. "You gonna give me more than this for my twenty dollars. Shit, if it's all like that I'll go to somebody else." She stared right into his face during her complaining, and quickly looked down at the ground when she was done. Alley Cat hated staring into her son's face because he looked exactly like his dad. Gusto's mom was raped in a park when she was a teenager by a wild looking Jamaican man. She was very scared and embarrassed after it happened and therefore chose to keep silent. But as time passed, her belly began to grow, and that's when she realized she was pregnant. Her relatives noticed as well and questioned her, but she would never tell them what happened on that tragic day. By the time her family took her to get an abortion, it was too late. She had no other choice but to keep the baby. Even until this day, Alley Cat kept the traumatizing incident silent. Gusto was not concerned with his mother's threat to take her business else where. "I got the best shit on this side of town, fuck wrong with you. If you go see somebody else, you'll be cheating yourself." Gusto still dropped another piece of crack in to his mother's hand.

Gusto hated his mother just as bad as she hated looking at him. When he was just seven years old, she sold him for an ounce of cocaine to a big time Haitian drug dealer named J.T. J.T. couldn't wait to put the young boy to work. By the time Gusto was fourteen, he moved up in rank after his boss took a liking to his cocky attitude and strict work ethic. As time went on, J.T. continued to put his trust

6

in Gusto and kept him close, showing him all the tricks and trades of the game. Little did he know, Gusto's heart grew colder with each year he worked for him. Gusto never got over the business transaction made between his mother and J.T. One day Gusto tried to rob J.T for his entire stash, but in the midst of things, J.T.'s right hand man Murder Max ran up on the robbery and sliced Gusto's throat in an attempt to kill him. This left Gusto with no choice but to kill Murder Max and J.T. And that's exactly what he did! Once J.T., the head of the organization, was knocked off, the drug movement relocated to a different town. Every once and a while, members from the old organization would pop up unexpectedly on Gusto trying to avenge their slain leader's death. It didn't matter, because Gusto was always on point and moved strategically while in the streets, knowing that his enemies would not rest until he was dead.

Alley Cat handed over a wrinkled twenty dollar bill. "Boy here", she stated. Noticing how fast his mother was trying to rush out of the alley way, Gusto yelled out, "This shit better be real." He stuffed the twenty in his front pocket, and turned to put back his stash. Once he was finished, he started to make his way out of the alley when he heard a noise. He turned to see where the noise was coming from. Immediately Gusto's eyes grew wide as he stopped in his tracks throwing his hands in the air. There was a short masked man dressed in all black, pointing a chrome long nose 38 revolver at Gusto's mid section. "Make the wrong move and I'm going to blow your fucking head off!" At first, Gusto's heart skipped a beat, but when he noticed the robber's shaky hand and the timid look in his eyes, he regained his composure. "I wish I would let this bitch ass nigga rob me in my own hood. Fuck that, bitch I'm Gusto", he bravely thought to himself as he continued to stare into the man's eyes, trying to break him. "What the fuck you standing there for? Empty your pockets, and give me all your jewelry!" "I ain't giving you shit!" Gusto reached his

7

hand out and tried to grip up the masked man. The two tussled over the gun, but before Gusto could get a good strong grip, the masked man broke loose. BLOW! BLOW! Gun fire sparked through the barrel of the gun as he aimlessly shot in Gusto's direction. "Ughh!" Gusto grunted in agony as he stumbled backwards, watching the gunman run off in the opposite direction. A burning sensation pierced through his right arm and his ear began stinging like hell. Large amounts of blood leaked all over his white shirt. Immediately, Gusto's survival instincts started to kick in. He put his hand over the bloody bullet wound in his arm, and stumbled out of the alley way.

Everyone on the block heard the shots ring out, so by the time Gusto made it out into the open there were several people already coming towards him. "Hurry up and take me to the hospital", Gusto stated before falling to the pavement. He fell on the side of a black mini van that was parked on the curb. Seeing the blood soaked shirt and Gusto's condition caused some of the bystanders to freeze in shock as they stood over top of him. "What y'all standing there for? Help me!" Gusto managed to plead for help in between deep breaths, as the blood continued to pour from his wounds. "Gusto calm down. I got you!" A tall, dark skin crack head named Hook Dog slid open the door to the black mini van. Two other people picked Gusto from off the ground and put him inside the van. Hook Dog closed the door, jumped behind the wheel, and sped off towards the hospital.

Alley Cat knew her son just got shot, but instead of rushing to the hospital to be by his side, she waited anxiously for the street to clear. Once the crowd died down, she snuck back in to the alley way and went straight to where she saw her son stash his crack. After snatching the stash, Alley Cat went to have a crack party with her friends.

CHAPTER 2: WHERE'S CHAMELEON?

The very next day, Gusto laid in the hospital bed shirtless watching television. There were several monitors hooked up to his body, a cast covering his right arm, and a huge bandage on his right ear. The bullet that pierced his arm traveled straight through, and even though the second bullet only caused a graze wound, Gusto still lost a huge chunk of his ear from it. He also lost several pounds because of the large amount of blood that left his body. But in spite of all that, he was still alive, functional, and well. His spirits were really lifted after the beautiful female nurse came in to tell him that he would be able to leave the hospital after the doctors ran a few more tests.

While waiting for the official okay to leave, Gusto entertained his visitors; his two young boys Lil Petey and Chopo, his girlfriend's best friend Shaky, and a few other people from his hood that came to show their love. Gusto's mother, and girlfriend Chameleon were the only two that were not there. Gusto still managed to make light of the life threatening incident that took place less than 24 hours ago. "I'm telling y'all man", Gusto looked around to make sure he had everyone's attention. "All I heard was foot steps creeping up behind me, but when I turned around I ain't see nobody. I thought I was loosing my mind until I heard him say he was going to blow my head off. That's when I looked down and saw the little muhfucka pointing his gun at me", he stated in a joking manner. The people in the room started laughing. Shaky, who was sitting in the chair next to Gusto's bed, had a pretty brown skin tone and rocked a stylish short hair cut. She was about five foot two with a well proportioned frame. For those that didn't know her personally would rate her a 7, but because of her caring nature and ride or die attitude she was a straight 10 to those who did know her. Plus she stayed fresh and had a swag out of this world.

"It was already bad enough I was getting robbed in my own hood, but damn, by a fucking dwarf though! That's when I tried to put this little nigga in a headlock, but he was so small I couldn't get a good grip on his ass. Next thing I know, he let off two shots. The scary nigga wasn't even looking when he did it." Gusto joined in with all the laughter that filled the room. Even though everyone was laughing, they all knew damn well the person responsible for last night's event was as dead as a door knob. "What the fuck is taking Geronimo so long to get here?", Chopo said in a low tone mostly to himself. Chopo was a skinny, six foot brown skin 17 year old pretty boy. His neatly done dreadlocks hung shoulder length, and his goatee was sharply lined. All he wanted to do was get money, stay fresh, and have his way with the ladies. "I don't know, call him and find out", Lil Petey responded with a slight attitude. While everyone else in the room found Gusto's jokes to be amusing, Lil Petey didn't find them funny at all. The thought of someone trying to take out the only older nigga in the hood that ever showed him love and kept a lil bit of money in his pocket, left a very bad taste in his mouth. He was no killer, but he damn sure was ready to become one! At the age of 16, Lil Petey was only about five foot one, but was extremely muscular. He had a low hair cut and no facial hair, which gave his dark skin an undeniable shine. Lil Petey and Chopo shared many of the same traits, and had a lot of things in common: chasing money, fucking bitches, and staying fly. That's what drew them to one another when they first met in middle school, and the two been rolling together every since. The only real difference between them was that Chopo was more relaxed and collected, while Lil Petey was on the thuggish side and often times walked around with a chip on his shoulder.

Without paying his friends smart remark any mind, a smirk appeared on Chopo's face. He knew his roll dog had a Neapolean complex. "Yeah, you right." Chopo pulled out his cell and began dialing Geronimo's number, but there was no answer. "Now this nigga ain't picking up his phone." Chopo spoke to Geronimo about an hour ago when he said he was ten minutes away, and now he wasn't even picking up his phone. "Ain't no telling…" Before Lil Petey could finish his sentence, Gusto's room door swung open, crashing against the wall, making a loud thump sound. Everyone in the room stopped to look at Geronimo and a tall skinny neighborhood crack head named Shitty Bitty rush into the room. "Here he go all dramatic and shit. And why the fuck he come with Itty Bitty?", Lil Petey thought to himself while watching the two approach Gusto's bedside. "You alright?", Geronimo asked. Itty Bitty stood behind Geronimo staring at Gusto with his big yellow eyes. Geronimo was Gusto's right hand man since the age of twelve. He was six foot three, with a stocky build and broad shoulders. His wheat bread skin complexion, thick eye brows, and curly braided corn rows gave him a foreign look. But Geronimo was 100% African American born and raised in the slums of Trenton, N.J. He was so animated, a picture of his face should have been next to the word in the dictionary. He was loud and loved attention, and had a fly swagger about himself. The way he fronted and stunted, you would think he was doing it for tv. Even at his worst he made it appear as if he was on top! He was a drama free type dude when it came to violence, even though he would always act like he was ready for war. When shit really hit the fan, he left all the wild cowboy shit up to Gusto.

"Yeah, I'm good", Gusto responded, smirking because he knew his right hand man always over played his role. "What happened?", Geronimo asked. "Some fuck boy tried to stick me up in the alley way. I tried to take the gun from him, but the scary nigga shot me and ran off." "Oh yeah?" Geronimo glanced back at Itty Bitty. "Which way did he run in the alley way?" Geronimo was trying to match Gusto's story with the one Itty Bitty told him. "He had to run straight on Sweets Ave, unless he cut through somebody's back yard. Why? What's up?" Gusto began getting curious, and began staring at Itty Bitty up and down. Geronimo was about to speak, but caught himself when he noticed the intense silence in the room. Everyone was all up in their conversation. "Goddamn man", Geronimo exclaimed in a high tone, throwing his hands in the air. "A yo, everybody step in the hallway real quick. Me and my brother about to discuss some things." Without saying a word, everyone got up from their seats and exited the room, everyone except Chopo and Lil Petey. "What the fuck y'all two still sitting down for? I..." Before Geronimo could finish his sentence, Gusto said, "Chill out bro, they good. They been holding me down the whole time I been in here." Gusto had been giving the two young boys coke to see what they were capable of, but never let them all the way inside the circle. This is why Geronimo reacted in such a hostile manner towards them. "Oh, alright." Geronimo eased up on the two, and then turned around and tapped Itty Bitty on the chest. "Now tell Gusto exactly what you told me", he demanded as he folded his arms across his chest, anticipating Gusto's reaction.

"I was on Sweets Avenue last night when you got shot and saw some little short dude wearing a mask run out of the alley. He jumped in a silver Buick, and right before he pulled off, he took off his mask and I saw his face." "Who was it?", Gusto was on the edge of his seat when a devilish look appeared on his face. "I don't know if you know him or not, but it was J Sky from North 25", Itty Bitty told him. J Sky was some dirty little young boy that lived around the corner and up the street from Sweets Ave in an apartment complex called North 25. He copped coke off Gusto once a week, but never bought over 10 grams during the few years they dealt with each other. "Wait, what?" Gusto couldn't believe it, and the way his face was twisted up said it all. He couldn't believe a clown like J Sky would have the balls to try his chin. Suddenly, the room door opened. It was Chopo and Lil Petey leaving out. "Yeah, it was him. I saw him with my own eyes", Itty Bitty reassured, putting extra emphasis on his words. "So what you want to do?", Geronimo asked. Gusto started breathing heavily from his nose, slowly letting out the steam that was building up. "You already know. It ain't too much more to talk about. The doctor said they was going to let me leave today. I wish they would hurry up, especially now that I know what I know." Gusto was ready to handle his handle. "Where's Chameleon?" Geronimo remembered he didn't see her in the room before telling everyone to leave. "When I spoke to her yesterday, she told me she was going to visit her aunt in Philly. She should be back in a few days." "So she don't know you got hit up?" "Nah, I tried to call her all this morning, but her phone when straight to voicemail", Gusto replied. "That bitch ain't at her aunt house", Geronimo thought to himself. He was disappointed in Gusto for believing that bullshit. "I'm about to call her right now to see if she pick up." Geronimo pulled his cell phone from his pocket and dialed Chameleon's number to see if she would answer for him, but just like Gusto said, the call when straight to voicemail.

CHAPTER 3: LET'S GET BIZZY

Meanwhile, Chameleon was at her aunt's house in Philly...Yeah right! That's just what she told Gusto so she could dip off with her cash cow for a few days. Truth of the matter is, Gusto was so blindly in love that he couldn't see through her lies. At this very moment Chameleon was in a luxurious 5 star hotel ass naked and bent over on all fours on an extremely plush king size bed getting hit from the back by her secret lover. "Oooh yeah. Oooh Bizzy! Fuck this pussy!" Chameleon moaned out as loud as she could, throwing her big soft ghetto booty back, meeting Young Bizzy with every short stroke. Chameleon was five foot three, and thick as a bowl of cold grits. She had silky jet black hair that came down to her shoulders. Her eyes's were sharply slanted and her smooth chocolate skin resembled a dark chocolate candy bar. "Mmmmm. Fuck me harder!" Chameleon turned back to look at Young Bizzy from the corner of her eye. He was completely nude, covered in sweat, and was stroking as hard as he could. She almost burst in to laughter at the sight of his ridiculous facial expressions and his fat and sloppy body jiggling just as much as her soft ass. "This yellow, fat, little dick muhfucka better hurry up and bust a nut", she thought to herself. In order to speed up the process, Chameleon started to throw her huge jiggly ass back even harder. Her wide chocolate ass began clapping loudly, sounding all throughout the room. CLAP! CLAP! CLAP! CLAP!

Chameleon's gigantic ass swallowed Young Bizzys's small penis. It was to the point where it felt like he was just grinding up against her. She definitely didn't have any problems slamming that pussy on him. "Ughhh! Oh shit!", he grunted as he tightly wrapped both of his chubby hands around her tiny waist, stroking her fiercely, drooling from his mouth and everything. The warm feeling of her wetness and the sight of her sweaty chocolate voluptious frame was

14

just too much to bare. It drove him wild! "It's about fucking time", Chameleon said to herself. Feeling his body tense up and seeing how hard he was going, she knew he was about to bust a nut, so she started talking dirty, knowing that he liked that. "You like this wet pussy and big juicy ass don't you? Now pull my hair and smack my ass!" Chameleon spoke in between fake moans, sounding like a straight up freak, looking back at Young Bizzy licking her tongue out. SMACK! SMACK! Young Bizzy did exactly what he was ordered to do. "Awwww yes! Just like that!" "Ughhh! I'm about to bust!" His body stiffened. "Agghhh! Shit!", he roared as thick globs of cum started to erupt from his small erect penis into her wetness.

Seconds later, Young Bizzy, still breathing heavy, pulled his manhood out of Chameleon's slit. "Damn that pussy good", he complimented sounding exhausted. Feeling drained, he flopped down on the bed and laid on his back with his arms spread out. Chameleon got out of the bed and walked to the bathroom, her booty jiggling with every step. "His fat ass breathing hard like he was really doing something", she thought to herself chuckling inside. She stepped in the all white bathroom, flicked the light switch on, and shut the door. While inside Chameleon grabbed a white hand towel and began to run water on it. She lifted her leg, placed it on the toilet lid, and started washing her cum dripping pussy. Once she was clean she stepped back into the room, only to find Young Bizzy snoring. She smirked knowing it was her wet pussy that put him to sleep.

Chameleon walked over to the bed and flopped down on it purposely to wake Young Bizzy. Young Bizzy's eyes slowly opened as a lazy smile crept across his fat face. "Baby what's up. You alright?", he stated as he rubbed his huge belly. Young Bizzy was the head man in charge of a drug organization that supplied majority of the city. He didn't earn his top spot like most of the other street bosses.

He got on heavy in the game from a lawsuit he received a few years ago. This was the only way a man like himself could have reached such a high level. Bizzy was soft and didn't have what it took to climb to the top of the food chain from the bottom of the barrel. "No! I'm not okay. Why you keep doing this to me?", Chameleon shot back as she began crying hysterically, burying her face in her hands. Young Bizzy quickly sat up. "What you talking about now?", he asked as he placed his hand on the back of her neck, rubbing it gently. "You keep fucking me raw, knowing I'm going to get pregnant and then you make me kill my baby", she whined in between sniffles. Chameleon was what you would call a money hungry, conniving, selfish, grimy, high priced hood rat that only gave the kitty cat up to dudes willing to spend big money on her. Yes she was in a deep relationship with Gusto, but that didn't stop her! She just couldn't help herself.

"The doctor said if I keep getting abortions it could fuck up my body. You don't even care about my health!" Chameleon was faking her ass off, knowing damn well she couldn't get pregnant because she was on birth control. She always lied to Young Bizzy so she could get whatever she wanted, and she used this particular tactic every few months. Young Bizzy sighed deeply as a strong feeling of guilt came over him. "Nah baby. It ain't even like that. When we first started fucking around we came up with an understanding. You knew your position, and was alright with it. Now you..." Before he could finish his sentence, she cut him off. "Yeah that's before you started fucking me raw and getting me pregnant. Everything changed once that happened! Now we killing my babies and fucking up my body!", she began crying again.

When Young Bizzy and Chameleon first started seeing each other, about 18 months ago, the two established a firm understanding that she was to be and remain his silent mistress with certain benefits. Chameleon knew

Young Bizzy was still in a serious relationship with his babymom, but once they started having unprotected sex she began to manipulate the entire situation. "Boy you just bust a nut inside of me a couple minutes ago. You know I get pregnant easy." Chameleon kept at it. Not really knowing what to say or do, Young Bizzy ran his hand over the top of his head and sighed. "Damn man. She got me on some other shit right now", he thought to himself. "Did you make your babymom keep getting abortions before she had your child?" Chameleon waited for his response for a few seconds, but he remained silent. "Don't be trying to ignore me." "Come on now Chameleon. We ain't got to go there. You belong to that little nigga Gusto." "That's only because you don't want to be with me." "What do you mean?", Young Bizzy started to raise his voice. He was getting fed up, but quickly caught himself and lowered his tone. "I am with you. It's just in a different way, that's all." "Yeah, very different!". Chameleon made sure she emphasized every word as she swung her neck from side to side, all ghetto with it. "You treat her way better than me. Only time you call me is when you want some pussy." Young Bizzy frowned, "No I don't!" "Yes you do!" The two were staring each other in the face. "No I don't!" "Yes you do!" Chameleon continued to scream to the top of her lungs as she stood over top of him with her fists balled up. "Calm down!" Young Bizzy quickly grabbed both of her arms, trying to prevent her from swinging.

Lil Petey, who was wearing a black ski mask half way over his head with a black long nose 357 on his lap, sat quietly and calmly in the passenger seat of a 2002 silver Buick with dark tented windows. He was bobbing his head to the 2pac lyrics that were pumping through the speakers while Chopo drove down Calhoun Street towards North 25. After hearing Itty Bitty tell the tale of the person who tried to take Gusto's life, Lil Petey made Chopo take him to go

17

settle the score. Lil Petey already knew everything about J Sky because they went to the same school, and was also familiar with the place in which he earned his crumbs.

Chopo started to have a bad feeling about Lil Petey's plot, and tried to talk him out of it. Lil Petey wasn't trying to hear it, to him it was the perfect opportunity to show his big dog that not only was he a go hard hustler, but he was also ready for action and was willing to play for keeps in the ice cold streets of Trenton. "Speed up so we won't get caught at the light", Lil Petey demanded. He was ready to get the task done so he could hit the strip and get back to the money. Chopo made it pass the traffic light, and continued to drive further down Calhoun Street. Finally, they made a left turn inside North 25 housing complex, slowly driving over the yellow speed bumps. North 25 was a small red brick apartment complex with two story buildings connected to one another. It looked somewhat like a small maze with three different ways to enter and exit. A basketball court was on one side of the complex, with a park was on the the opposite end.

Chopo slowly drove through the parking lot, allowing Lil Petey to prowl the area in search for his target. He saw a few young men in front of the basketball court playing ball, this was expected because of the warm weather on such a hot summer evening. He continued to scan. "Oh shit, there go that bitch ass nigga right there!" Lil Chopo spotted J Sky sitting in the driver's seat of his black Honda, parked near a dumpster in between the two buildings that led to the other side of the complex. J Sky had his head down and was not paying any attention to his surroundings, he was busy counting money and getting ready to bag up some coke. Chopo swallowed hard, the whole ride he was hoping that J Sky wouldn't be out. "Drive around the other side of the parking lot", Lil Petey demanded. Chopo did exactly that, he drove pass J Sky, and backed up in to a parking spot. "Keep the car running. Don't even put it in

18

park, just keep your foot on the break." Lil Petey got ready to get out the car, while Chopo looked around noticing all the people that were standing in front of the buildings. "Man its too many people out here." Chopo was still trying to stop the hit from going down. "Fuck that!", Lil Petey growled with clenched teeth, still focused on the enemy. He then pulled his ski mask down to cover his face, grabbed his 357 magnum, and climbed out of the car. Lil Petey began running through the walkway, everyone standing around immediately stopped what they were doing and watched in fear, knowing something bad was about to happen. As soon as Lil Petey got near the green dumpster, he slowed down and crept around it. He stopped at the edge of the dumpster, and peeked around it to make sure J Sky was still in the same position. Once he had confirmed he had the drop on his target, Lil Petey rushed towards him with his gun drawn and jumped on the hood of J Sky's car. J Sky, looked up with fear in his eyes, he was in complete shock. BOOM! BOOM! BOOM! BOOM! BOOM! BOOM! Before J Sky could make a move, Lil Petey sent all six slugs crashing through the front windshield, striking J Sky in his chest and stomach. Lil Petey succeeded, J Sky was killed instantly.

CHAPTER 4: TAYLA

Although it was still early in the day, North Trenton was still lively. Several young women were walking through the streets half dressed letting their skin show, street hustlers stood in front of the corner stores, and a few overcrowded dice games went on in front of some of the abandoned buildings. Geronimo cruised down Martin Luther King Boulevard in his black Cadillac with Gusto sitting quietly in the passenger seat observing all those who occupied the streets. Everyone in the hood already heard about what happened to him the night before, so they were surprised to see him out of the hospital so soon. "Damn, you see that little bad bitch right there!", Gusto exclaimed. He became excited when he spotted the unfamiliar young female exiting the New Way mini market.

Geronimo immediately took his eye's off the road and looked to see who caught Gusto's attention. "Yeah she nice." "Hurry up and whip down on her." Geronimo slowly pulled up on the female, while Gusto rolled down his window and stuck his head out. "What's up babes? Let me holla at you real quick." Gusto tried to be smooth by licking his full lips. "Damn she sexy", he thought has he admired her physical appearance. The young female was wearing a white and burgandy, tightly fitted dress that exposed her smooth caramel skin. She was about five foot six, and had a petite, but very curvacious frame. Her silky brown hair dropped a little pass her shoulder, and blended with her skin tone.

She turned her head and smirked when she saw Gusto's handsome face and light brown eyes. Gusto picked up on it, and at that moment he knew she wasn't going to be hard to bag. Geronimo put the car in park to let his friend get out. The young female noticed the cast on his arm and bandage on his ear. "Damn, what the hell happened to him?", she wondered. "I been living around here all my life

20

and never seen you. You must not be from around here",
Gusto said. "Umm, that's funny because I been living
around here all my life too, and this the first time I'm seeing
you." "Word up! That mean I'm slipping then. You been
living around here all this time and I'm just now seeing you.
I should just slap myself", Gusto replied in a joking way,
trying to be charismatic. He ran through damn near every
bad broad in the hood, so for him to hear what he just heard
was shocking to him. The young female began laughing,
revealing her crystal white teeth. "Why you say you should
slap yourself?" She glanced at Geronimo who was still in
the car, staring directly at her. "Because I would have been
tried to do what I'm trying to do now." "And what's that?",
she asked looking deep into his eyes. "Make you mines."
"Oh really? That's cute, but you seem kind of rough", she
stated trying to hold back her smile. "Who me? Nah, I be
kicked back laid back. Focused on the paper." "Well what
happened to your arm?" "It's a long story", Gusto replied.
He could tell she wasn't a street type of girl, so he didn't
want to tell her what happened and risk scaring her away.
"I don't have anywhere important to go. I'm all ears", she
insisted. Gusto took a deep breath before speaking, "Some
stick up kid tried to rob me, and when I tried to take the gun
from him he shot me." Her eyes grew wide. "He tried to
kill you? Do you know who did it?", she was concerned and
surprised that someone would do such a thing. "Nah.
Anyway, we been talking all this time and I don't even know
your name", Gusto proceeded to change the subject. "My
name is Tayla. What's yours?" Tayla was impressed by
Gusto's bravery, but could tell he didn't want to talk about
his wounds, so she decided to drop the subject, for now.
"My name Gusto. So what's up, are you going to let me get
your number so I can come scoop you one day and show
you how to have some fun?" Tayla smirked. "Show me
how to have some fun huh. It depends on what type of fun
you talking about." In a very cool manner, Gusto folded his

21

arms across his chest. "I'm talking about the kind of fun when you decide what you want to do and I make it happen", he stated cockily. "This boy is too damn much", Tayla thought to herself. Although her mother always told her not to mess around with young men caught up in the street life, Tayla wanted to see what Gusto was about. His fly boy, thuggish swag was totally different from the boys in her school, who often acted as if they were too intimidated by her beauty. Tayla pulled out her cell phone, while Gusto pulled out his. The two exchanged numbers. "Alright. I'll probably call you tomorrow night or something", he told her. "That's cool." Gusto turned to walk back to the car and Tayla went to hers, pulling off.

Once he was back in the car, Gusto told Geronimo to cut through the alleyway on Midrose so he could grab his stash. Geronimo pulled off eventually making it to the alleyway. As he drove deeper into the alley, Gusto noticed a dark skin heavy set man serving two female fiends coke. "Who the fuck is this nigga busting a trap in my alleyway?" Geronimo spotted the heavy set young man making the transaction, but didn't recognize his face. "I don't know who this fat fuck head is!" "You don't know him either. Well he about to find out who we is", Gusto replied. He slipped his hand underneath his white T shirt and pulled a blue steel beretta from off his waistband. "Stop the car." Immediately Geronimo stopped the car, Gusto climbed out and rushed towards the young man hustling in his territory. The fiends noticed Gusto and the crazed look in his eyes along with the shiny piece of steel in his hand, and backed away in fear. "Who the fuck gave you the okay to be in my alley selling coke?" Gusto spoke with clenched teeth, and at the same time swung as hard as he could, violently smacking the intruder in the nose with the butt of the gun. CRACK! The young man didn't know what hit him, all he felt was his nose bone crack and began seeing stars. Blood started pouring like a faucet all over his crispy white t-shirt, dripping down to his air forces. The young man tried to grab his nose to stop the blood from pouring. "Man you broke my nose!", he stated in a muffled tone, holding his hand over his nose and mouth.

Geronimo stood in front of the car a few feet away from Gusto with his arms folded across his chest and a blank expression on his face. Deep inside, he was really hoping Gusto didn't take it any further than he already did. But, in a split second, his hopes were shattered. BLOW! A spark of fire came from the gun. Gusto shot the intruder in the ass. "Now get the fuck from around here!" "Agghh!", the man screamed in agony as he staggered forward. The hot bullet pierced his right but cheek, which caused a burning sensation to travel down to his right foot. Screaming like a bitch, he rushed out of the alley way leaving trails of blood along the dirty ground. "We better not see your bitch ass around here again!", Geronimo chimed in, adding his two cents. Gusto pointed the gun towards the gate where his stash was. "Hop over and grab my stash from underneath the wooden board." Geronimo jumped the gate, and lifted the board, but didn't see anything. "A yo. It ain't nothing under the board big bro." Geronimo dropped the board back down, and started walking back towards the gate. Gusto twisted up his face, he couldn't believe it. "It ain't nothing under the board?" "Nah, somebody probably stole it", Geronimo stated plainly. He quickly hopped back over the fence, and the two of them got back in to the car and pulled off. "Damn! Why the fuck all this bullshit keep happening to me like this? First I got shot the fuck up, then I catch some clown ass nigga trying to get money in my alley. Now I find out that somebody stole my fucking work. What I got cold blooded sucker written over my face?"

Once at the end of the alley, Gusto saw his mother standing on the sidewalk next to an old dusty white Honda Accord. Suddenly, he remembered that she saw where he hid his stash when he was serving her earlier. "That nappy head muhfucka probably stole my shit", he thought to himself. "Whip down on my mom real quick. I gotta ask her something!" Geronimo pulled up on Alley Cat. Gusto got out of the car. Alley Cat saw her son coming towards her, and knew he knew that she saw where he stashed his drugs. She wore an oversized dingy white t-shirt that had Fubu in big bold red letters written on it. She already had her statement prepared for her son. "You stole my fucking coke last night?" Gusto stopped in his tracks, towering over her. "Boy don't be walking up on me like that!", she shot back. Small particles of spit flew out of the toothless gaps in her mouth. "You must have lost your damn mind!" Alley Cat pushed her son a few feet back to remove him from her face. "And don't be accusing me of stealing your coke boy! When I heard the shots I ran off and was so scared that I didn't even realize I made it all the way out West Trenton. But anyway. Are you alright?" Gusto didn't believe one word of his mother's story. "Man you don't give a fuck about me!", he barked harshly. Alley Cat looked down at the ground. "Come on now Gusto, your my son. I was going to come to the hospital to check up on you but I got warrants." Gusto couldn't do nothing but shake his head. "They don't do warrant checks at the hospital!" He knew his mother all too well; she was a tactical thief, a habitual liar, and had more game than a little bit. The only problem with this current situation, was that he couldn't prove she did it, just like every other time she stole from him.

The loud sound of a car horn echoed throughout the air. BEEP! BEEP! Gusto turned and saw Chopo and Lil Petey in a green Pontiac pulling up behind where Geronimo was parked. "Big bro, I gotta holly at you. It's real important", Lil Petey yelled out the passenger side window. Gusto could tell by the look on Lil Petey's face, that he was holding some real serious information. Gusto left his mother where she stood and started walking towards his two young boys. "Park the car and meet me in the trap house", Gusto instructed Chopo and Geronimo as he made his way down the street towards a red brick house. This was the house Gusto used to move his work out of sometimes. It was owned by an older man named Slick. Slick was a smoker, so he only charged Gusto a small fee to use his house. And even though there was a lot of traffic in and out, they managed to keep it fairly clean. The living room was furnished with a dingy grey rug situated in the center of the floor, a worn down black suede sofa and love seat occupied most of the space, and a small 25 inch tv sat on a wooden table that was pushed up against the wall.

Gusto was already seated on the sofa by the time Geronimo, Chopo, and Lil Petey walked through the front door. They all sat down. "So what's so important ya'll got to tell me?", Gusto asked as he pulled a perfectly rolled blunt of haze out of his pocket. Lil Petey looked over his shoulder towards the kitchen to make sure no one was in the house. Gusto smirked. "Ain't nobody in her lil bro. I already checked. Geronimo, let me get a light." Geronimo struck his lighter and held the fire towards Gusto's blunt until it was lit. Gusto took a deep pull, and then exhaled the smoke from his nose. Knowing the type of person Geronimo was, Lil Petey was hesitant in telling Gusto about the work he just put in, but knew he couldn't hold it any longer. "Me and Chopo caught that bitch ass nigga J Sky slipping and bust his ass", he said proudly, waiting for Gusto's reaction. Gusto's eyebrows rose. "Word up!" Gusto knew the two fly young boys were able to scrape up some change, but never in a million years would he have thought they were about gun play too. "Yeah, we caught him sitting in his car in North 25. I think he dead too", Lil Petey continued. "These little young punks ain't built like that", Geronimo thought to himself as jealousy pierced his heart. Every since he was a young boy he wished he had the balls to put in some real work like Lil Petey and Chopo just did, but it wasn't in him. "What you mean you think the nigga dead?! If yawl really bust the nigga ass y'all would know for sure if he was dead or not!", Geronimo stated sounding overly excited.

Without taking his eyes off Lil Petey, Gusto motioned his hand for Geronimo to be quiet. "Chill out bro." Geronimo closed his mouth and sat back down. Gusto glanced at Chopo, who was playing in his dreads. "So who was the shooter?" Lil Petey gave Gusto a sly look to let him know it was him. A wicked grin spread across Gusto's face as he chuckled, taking another pull from his blunt. "And the best thing about it is you was in the hospital. So if worse came to worse, they can't link you up on nothing", Lil Petey stated in a calm tone. Gusto was highly impressed by how thoroughly Lil Petey handled everything. He started replaying the entire day in his head. He remembered that Itty Bitty saw the two young boys when they left the hospital. "The only one who know about J Sky besides us is Itty. We got to keep him close." Everyone in the room agreed. Itty Bitty was well known throughout North Trenton, so he wouldn't be hard to find or to keep tabs on. "You want us to go find him and bring him here?", Chopo asked. "Nah, I got him. He ain't too far. Shit he probably right in the alleyway somewhere", Gusto replied. Lil Petey remembered there was something else he had to tell Gusto. "Oh yeah, we done with all that work you gave us big bro." The two young boys both pulled out a wad of cash, handing it to Gusto. Gusto didn't bother to count the money before stuffing it in his pocket. "We ready for some more", Chopo stated. "Give me a day or two, the last little bit I had somebody stole it." Geronimo gave Itty Bitty the last couple of grams he had, so it was definitely time to re-up. Gusto told his young boys that they were officially apart of the team and explained how he wanted to restructure things before he sent them on their way. He then sent Geronimo to find Itty Bitty and Hook Dog.

CHAPTER 5: SQUAD UP

After riding though every single block in North
Trenton, Geronimo finally spotted Itty Bitty on Sanford
Street washing a gray Lincoln Navigator. "There his black
ass go right there", Geronimo said to himself. He slowly
pulled up on Itty Bitty who had his back turned kneeling
down dipping a sponge in a bucket of soapy water. "What's
up you black muhfucka!" Itty Bitty was caught off guard, he
turned to see who startled him. "Don't be creeping up on
me like that. You scared the shit out of me man! A turd
damn near fell out my ass!" Geronimo couldn't help but
laugh. "Itty Bitty you shot out. Hurry up and get in the car
so we can take this ride to the spot. Gusto wanna talk to
you." Itty Bitty immediately stopped washing the car and
looked at Geronimo like he was crazy, taking a few steps
backwards. It looked like he was about to start running. "I
ain't getting in no car to go talk to nobody. I heard how that
young boy J Sky just got killed a few hours ago." Itty Bitty
been around for too long to fall for the *come take a ride with
me* trick. After hearing about J Sky's murder, he became
shook up and felt kind of bad. Shook because of how fast it
happened, and bad because he had lied about the whole
situation. Yeah, J Sky's murder was based on a lie Itty Bitty
told. He was on Sweets Avenue the night Gusto got shot,
but he never saw the shooter. The only reason he blamed
him was because a week earlier he got into a very heated
argument with J Sky who refused to serve him over four
dollars. Not only that, Geronimo was offering crack for a
story, so that's what he gave him. "What I look stupid? If
y'all think I'm going to tell somebody, I'm not. I don't know
nobody and I ain't see shit." "Awe man Itty Bitty stop it.
Ain't nobody on no bullshit like that. Get in the car." "Nah
dog. I got to finish washing this truck to get some money so
I can buy my medicine", he stated still looking like he was
about to make a run for it. "Damn you smoked all that shit I

gave you already?!" "Hell yeah", Itty Bitty shot back with white foam appearing in the corners of his mouth. "I been smoking crack since I was thirteen. I'm a certified crack head. I smoked those punk ass three grams you gave..." Geronimo cut him off, "Man look, if we was on some bullshit we wouldn't have came talking. We would've just left you stanking like that nigga J Sky." Itty Bitty stood there thinking about what Geronimo just said, and recognized the logic behind his words. He decided to get in the car. "Alright. I'll take this ride with you, but as soon as I see some funny shit I'm jumping out this bitch while it's moving." Itty Bitty dropped his rag and climbed inside the car. Geronimo started laughing as he took his foot off the brake and pulled off, as they were now in search of Hook Dog. The entire time they drove around Geronimo boasted and lied saying that he was the one who had J Sky killed for shooting Gusto. When they finally found Hook Dog, he stopped talking and took them both to the trap house where Gusto was waiting.

Everyone walked in the living room where Gusto was still seated on the sofa. "Damn, it's about time y'all got here. What took so long?" "It took me like a hour to find Itty Bitty, and another twenty minutes to talk his scary ass to get in the car", Geronimo explained while grabbing a seat. "I ain't fucking around with y'all crazy ass young boys. I ain't trying to die just yet. I like smoking crack too much." Itty Bitty might have sound funny, but he was very serious. Him and Hook Dog both sat down. Gusto could not stop laughing, he knew exactly what Itty Bitty was thinking. "Nah, Itty. It ain't like that. You family now." "Well shit, I hope so." Crook Dog remained silent, but was sitting too close to his fellow crack smoker. "Damn Hook Dog! What you about to do rub on my thigh and give me a kiss. Move the hell over some." Geronimo and Gusto got a kick out of the two. Hook Dog felt offended and embarrassed. "You better watch your mouth. I don't play that gay shit!", Hook

28

Dog stated while moving over. "I don't want to hear that tuff guy shit", Itty Bitty kept going. Hook Dog bit the bottom of his lip and balled up both of his fists. "What!" "Alright y'all. Chill out", Gusto finally broke it up.

The two still mumbled something slick to one another before they fixed their attention back on Gusto. "We're here to talk about how we going to get rich, and you two niggas about to get into it over some dumb shit. I don't even think y'all ready for what I wanted to put y'all up on", Gusto stated sounding upset. "Oh yes the hell I am. I ain't got no problem with Hook Dog!" Gusto turned to look at Hook Dog. "What about you?" "Nah, I ain't got no problem with Itty. He just talk to fucking much sometimes. I'm ready to get paid too", Hook Dog assured. "Alright then. I want y'all to stand on post and be lookouts for my workers in the alley from 6 o'clock in the evening until 2 o'clock in the morning. Before they leave the shift, they gonna to hit y'all off with twenty five grams a piece to hold the alley down with. When they come back the next day, give them every thing that was made and any work that's left. As of right now, y'all starting off with five hundred dollars a week. Once everything start moving how it's suppose to, y'all pay day will get even larger. That sound alright?" The two men were trying hard to hold back the grins that were trying to emerge on their face. Instead of speaking, they both shook their heads in agreement. The truth was Itty Bitty and Hook Dog had known each other for so long, so they wouldn't have too much of a problem working together. Well, at least that's what they hoped. "I hope you understand, because if any bullshit happens you know the consequences", Gusto was dead serious. The only reason he chose Hook Dog to work for him was to return the favor for taking him to the hospital when he got shot. "So when are we going to start?", Hook Dog asked eagerly. "Two days from now. So make sure you stay in the area", Geronimo answered, breaking his silence. "Oh don't worry, we'll be around. Matter fact, me and Hook Dog roll dogs for now on", Itty Bitty stated as he smiled, showing his yellow teeth. He turned to look at Hook Dog. "Now how bout that?" "Shit. I'm with it. Thats the way it's going to be then", Hook Dog agreed. "Alright. Y'all can leave now. See you in two days", Geronimo stated. Itty Bitty and Hook Dog stood up to leave. As they approached the door, they noticed the front door knob moving. They both looked back at Gusto and Geronimo. "Yo somebody trying to get up in here", Itty Bitty warned. Finally the door opened. It was the home owner, Talk Slick, walking through the door.

Talk Slick was about five foot seven, chubby, and had an extremely dry brown skin complexion with a nappy thick beard and low hair cut. As soon as he saw Itty Bitty walking towards him, the adrenaline in his body began to rush. Talk Slick threw a wild overhand punch, using all his might, striking Itty Bitty in the mouth, splitting it instantly. "Aghh!" Itty Bitty grunted as he stumbled backwards and fell to the floor. Without wasting another second, Talk Slick rushed over top of him and wrapped his huge crusty hands around Itty Bitty's skinny neck, and began choking the life out of him. With wide eyes and a bloody mouth, Itty Bitty grabbed hold to Talk Slick's big hands in an attempt to break loose, but the grip was too tight. He was also still dizzy from the punch. "Where the fuck my money at muhfucka?", Talk Slick growled harshly with clenched teeth, looking Itty Bitty in the face with crazed eyes. About three weeks prior, when Gusto ran out of coke, Talk Slick and Itty Bitty went half on a gram of coke so they could smoke and get high, but when Itty Bitty went to get cop, he never returned. Talk Slick began hunting him down since that day, but could never catch up with him, until now. "I said where the fuck my money at?"

Everything was happening so fast, the other three men in the room just watched in shock before they tried breaking up the scuffle. While Geronimo and Hook Dog rushed to grab Talk Slick off of Itty Bitty, Gusto stood up from the couch and grabbed his blue steal Beretta from his hip, aiming it towards the ceiling. BLOW! He let off a single shot, which echoed loudly throughout the house, and caused dust and ceiling particles to fall. "Get the fuck off him!" Immediately, everyone in the room stopped to look at Gusto, fearful of what he might do next. Itty Bitty slowly crawled over to the couch, placing his hand over the center of his chest as he gasped for air. "Now what the fuck is this about?", Gusto looked to Talk Slick for the answer. Talk Slick was breathing heavy, still trying to gain his composure. "I sent his bitch ass to go cop something for me that time you ran out of coke, and he ran off with my money." Slick's voice sounded raspy, as if he had dried up hog spit stuck in the middle of his throat. "How much was it?", Gusto asked. "Twenty five dollars." Slick started to wonder why Gusto was so concerned and taking up for Itty Bitty. "Geronimo, give him twenty dollars." Geronimo dug in his pocket and got out two crispy twenty dollar bills, handing them both to Talk Slick. "You good now?", Gusto questioned. "Yeah I'm good. Shit, I got my money back." Talk Slick glanced at Itty Bitty who was on the couch using his dirty shirt to wipe the blood from his mouth. "Alright now listen, Itty Bitty and Hook Dog work for me now. So whatever fallout you two had is officially over. We one big happy family now. Understand?" Slick was surprised and wanted to know what exactly was going on, but instead of causing problems for himself he just nodded his head in agreement. "Yeah, I understand." Itty Bitty stood up, "It's my fault, I ain't have no business running off with that man money. I apologize Slick." Itty Bitty would have offered him a handshake, but his hands were too bloody.

Gusto felt his cell phone vibrating in his pocket. "Who the fuck is this?", he thought to himself. He placed his smoking gun on the couch, and then grabbed his cell out his pocket. A smile appeared on his face when he read the incoming caller's name. It was Tayla. "Oh shit, she called quick", he thought. "Hello." "What's up Gusto! What you doing?", Tayla stated on the other end of the phone, sounding a little eager. "Nothing really, I just got finish setting a few things straight", he replied as he walked in the kitchen. The two stayed on the phone with one another for several hours joking, laughing, and getting familiar with one another. By the end of the call, they agreed to go out on a date.

CHAPTER 6: SHIT AIN'T ADDING UP

Geronimo stood on the corner of Trent and Calhoun streets holding a small duffle bag filled halfway with wads of cash, carefully observing his surroundings as several cars passed by. He was waiting for the connect to drop off the order he placed the night before. Whenever it was time to re-up, Gusto always sent him to make the transaction. Geronimo was definitely familiar with the procedure, but he began to grow impatient after realizing the connect was 10 minutes late. "Where the fuck this nigga at", Geronimo said to himself. He grabbed a black and mild cigar from out his ear and put it in his mouth, biting down on the plastic tube. He pulled out his lighter to light the cigar, in hopes it would help to calm his nerves. Geronimo took a deep pull, then released the smoke into the hot humid air. After a couple of pulls, he spotted a black Buick with dark tented windows cruising down Calhoun street towards him. "There his ass go right there." The car drove pass Geronimo to make left turn on Trent Street, and parked a couple houses from the corner. Geronimo flicked the last bit of his cigar on the street before making his way to the car. He got in. "What's good neph", the supplier Da'White said enthusiastically. He was black, but everyone called him Da'White because he looked like a white boy. He had light skin with straight jet black hair. Not only was Da'White the go to man in Young Biz's drug organization, he was also Young Bizzy's first cousin. The two cousins went from innocent children that loved playing video games, into certified hustlers that shared a strong bond. "Damn what took you so long?" Geronimo had a displeased look on his face after he closed the passenger door, now holding the duffle bag of money on his lap. "My fault, my babymom got on some bullshit because she ain't want me to leave the crib. So I had to put her in her place", he explained. "Alright man. Lets hurry this shit up." He unzipped the bag, revealing the wads of cash.

"You know my money good. It's all there." They been dealing with each other a little over a year, and Geronimo never came up short. Da'White trusted that everything was official. "Toss it in the back." Geronimo placed the bag in the back while Da'White reached underneath the driver's seat and grabbed a black book bag. "You said one bird and a half, right?" Da'White smirked as he handed the bag to Geronimo. "These lame ass niggas finally stepped it up a notch", he thought to himself. He knew Geronimo and Gusto were putting their money together to purchase a whole kilo. Da'White always looked at the two as petty corner hustlers that would never make it to his level. Not to mention, he also knew his cousin was having his filthy way with Gusto's main squeeze Chameleon, which made the situation even more comical to him.

Geronimo unzipped the bag, pulled out the square packages that were thoroughly wrapped in plastic, and began examining it. "Man I hope this shit good because you gave me some straight bullshit last time." "Nah, that ain't no bullshit. That's probably the best coke in town right now", Da'White stated. "You need me I don't need you fuck boy. You get whatever I decide to give you", he thought to himself. "Okay, I'ma take your word for it." Geronimo still had his doubts, but proceeded to put the blocks of cocaine back into the bag, zippering it up. "Oh shit. Don't move. There go that black car", Da'White warned nervously in a low tone as his heart began beating rapidly. Out of now where a black unmarked Caprice with two white cops in it pulled up beside Da'White's darkly tented vehicle. The driver began shining his flashlight inside the car, trying to see if anyone was in it. "Awe fuck", Geronimo thought to himself as fear gripped his heart, causing his entire body to tense up. The cops motioned as if they were about to get out of their vehicle, but became distracted by their walkie talkies. It just so happened there was a wild shoot out taking place around the corner, so instead they quickly sped off towards the action. Geronimo wasted no time, he quickly made his way to his car parked around the corner. Da'White pulled off and made his way out of the area.

When Geronimo walked through the front door, Gusto was already in the kitchen sitting in a chair waiting. He had everything prepared: glass plates, two boxes of plastics, two boxes of baking soda, a black digital scale, and a chrome long nose 357 Magnum. "That's you Geronimo?", Gusto yelled from the kitchen, grabbing his pistol from the table. "Yeah it's me." Geronimo locked the door behind him, and walked in the kitchen. "Man I thought you got bumped or something", Gusto stated sounding relieved. "I almost did. The black car whipped down on us, and started shining the flashlight in the car while he was serving. I thought it was over. Good thing that nigga got dark ass tents." "Word up?" "Hell yeah bro." Geronimo noticed that all the tools he needed was already laid out on the table. "Oh you got everything set up huh." "You already know. I'm ready to get this paper", Gusto stated anxiously. He lived for everything the street life had to offer, plus he couldn't wait to see how hard his workers was willing to go for the team. He really felt like he had a nice squad on his hands.

Geronimo placed the book bag on the table and unzipped it, pulling out the two huge blocks of cocaine. "Let me see it", Gusto stated. Geronimo handed Gusto one of the packages. Gusto placed the block on a round glass plate, grabbed a silver butter knife, and slowly cut straight down the middle. He then dug the knife in between the slit, and scooped up a small amount of substance and held it up close. "Man this look like the same stepped on bullshit that nigga sold us last time." "I said the same thing to him. He said it's different though. And probably the best coke in the city." "Oh yeah. Well we about to see. Grab a pot and cook it up." Geronimo walked over to the sink where he found a silver pot and proceeded to fill it with water. Once he felt he had enough, he turned the water off and made his way to the stove. He lit the fire on the gas range and placed the pot on the heat. Geronimo went to work like a chef, putting together his special recipe. Gusto was still working with his one good hand, he was responsible for weighing the product on the scale and bagging up. The goal was to bag a hundred grams a piece in each plastic bag.

A few hours had passed and the two were finally done. The potent smell of cooked crack roamed through the house. Gusto was still seated in the same position, neatly placing the 100 gram packages in rows of three on the table. He was counting them out loud for the second time to make sure his count was accurate, the first count seemed way to short. "Nine, ten, eleven, twelve." Gusto began to breath heavily out of his nose, as he looked over to a speechless Geronimo who was staring back at him. Gusto slammed his fist on the table. "This only twelve hundred fucking grams! And this shit ain't no where near cooked to the oil!" Every time they cooked up a key of coke they would bring back 14 hundred grams of good crack, which always left them with an extra two hundred grams to split equally. This time they purchased more and produced less. Geronimo was sick with the outcome. "You see it with your own eyes", Gusto stated motioning his hand at the bagged up crack on the table. "I'm about to call Da'White bitch ass right now." Just as Geronimo reached for his phone, Gusto stopped him. "Nah, don't call that nigga. This ain't the first or second time those fuck boys served us some bullshit ass coke. They know what the hell they doing so fuck it! We gonna wait a few days, and call him up for two keys. Then whack that pussy for it." "But then where we gonna get our coke from", Geronimo started focusing on the business. "My cousin Butchy from Wilbur Section", Gusto had all the answers. He used to do business with his cousin Butchy a while back, but stopped because he too started selling him bullshit coke. It wasn't as bad as what he was getting from Da'White the last month and a half, so he figured he was better off doing business with his peoples.

Gusto felt his cell phone vibrating. He was still thinking about the bad deal, he answered it without even checking to see who it was. "Hello." "What's up baby. Where you at?", Chameleon asked. "What you mean where I'm at. Where the hell you at?", Gusto replied in a hostile tone. "Come on now Gusto, I already told you I was going to my aunt's house in Philly." "Then why the hell you had your phone off for these last couple days?" "Baby, my phone was off because I lost it. I had to buy a brand new phone and everything. They let me keep my same number though", Chameleon lied. The reason why she had a brand new cell phone is because Young Biz bought her one, along with all the other gifts he got her when he took her shopping. "Oh so somebody stole your phone huh?", Gusto responded in a sarcastic tone. "Yeah! I lost my phone! Don't nobody got to lie to you. Shit, you'll see the new phone when I see you, where you at?" "I'm on Fountain Avenue." "Well hurry up and come to the house, I'll be there in a few minutes", she told him. "I'm on my way right now", Gusto finally gave in. Once he hung up the phone, he told Geronimo "I'll be right back, I'm about to go to the crib real quick. Oh yeah, go find everybody so we could get things moving." The both of them left the house and went their separate ways.

A yellow taxi cab turned off the boulevard and began driving up Fountain Avenue. Chameleon was in the backseat looking out the window at some of the people on the street. "That will be five dollars", the white heavy set cabbie stated politely as he finished his drive up the steep hill. Chameleon reached in her purse and pulled out a ten dollar bill. "Here you go sir, but I'm only dropping these bags off here. I need for you to drop me off at 55 Sweets. Just give me a minute." The cab driver nodded, stuffing the money in his pocket. "Can you please beep the horn and pop the trunk", she asked. The driver did just that, allowing Chameleon to grab her bags from the trunk. "Shaky come help me with all these bags!" Chameleon began walking towards the house with both of her hands full with shopping bags. Shaky came out to help her friend, and carried some of her bags in the house. "Girl why the hell you had your phone off for all those days? I was calling you like crazy", Shaky didn't appreciate her friends absence either. "I don't know why, you knew who I was with." "I was calling because I sold all the weed we had left, and needed more." "Damn you sold all that wed already", Chameleon was surprised at her friends hustling skills. "Yeah girl, money was coming like crazy after I ran out too. But we missed it all." "Nah bitch, I ain't miss a goddamn thing. You missed out on the money", Chameleon said to herself selfishly, as she thought about her recent shopping spree and the three stacks Young Biz just gave her. "Damn Shaky, my bad girl", Chameleon apologized. "Go get what you made so I can get us some more weed." Chameleon went upstairs to get the money. "Hurry up. I got Gusto waiting for me at the house. I need you to keep these clothes here for me cause if he see all these bags he gonna be on some bullshit." Shaky came back down the stairs carrying a dark blue gym bag, handing it to Chameleon. Here you go. There's sixty five hundred inside for a pound of haze. Your profit is in the little pocket on the side." "Alright, see you later", Chameleon stated as she rushed out of the house and got back into the taxi cab. Shaky forgot to tell her that Gusto got shot.

The bright yellow cab drove down Sweets Avenue. Chameleon saw Gusto sitting on the concrete steps that led to their porch. Just before the driver made it to her house, she told him to "Stop right here." The driver stopped the car, allowing her to get out. "Alright miss, have a good one." "You too", Chameleon replied as she hopped out, closing the door behind her. Gusto stood up and stepped off the porch. Chameleon's eyes grew wide, she was in shock when she saw that Gusto had a cast on his arm and a bandage on his ear. "Baby what happened?" Gusto twisted his face up, "If your ass didn't have your phone off when I tried to call you, you would know." Chameleon squinted her eyes as she snapped back. "I told you, I lost my phone and had to buy a new one!" "Where is it then?" Chameleon made a loud sigh as she pulled her phone out her purse, holding it up to Gusto's face. "You see it! Brand! New! Phone!" When Gusto saw her proof, he felt guilty for being suspicious and coming at his girl's neck. "Alright man. Calm down, that's my fault." "Why you always think I'm lying to you, or doing some bullshit behind your back. I really love you", she whined as if she was about to cry. Chameleon gave Gusto a warm hug, holding on to him before she softly kissed him on his neck and face. "Now tell me what happened to you."

Gusto started to explain to her what happened. While he was deep in his story, Young Bizzy made a left turn on the block in his Pepsi blue BMW convertible with the top down bobbing his head to the Nas lyrics that blared through his speakers. The music was so loud, it echoed throughout the entire street, causing everyone to stop and stare at him. When Young Bizzy saw Gusto and Chameleon hugged up, he laughed as he slowly drover closer. He found it quite amusing to see them on some husband and wife type shit, knowing she was with him for the past few days. Chameleon got nervous as she watched Young Biz drive towards them. Hearing the loud music and feeling Chameleon's body tense up, Gusto broke loose from her hold and turned around. "What the fuck is so funny", Gusto thought to himself noticing a smile on his new enemy's face. Seeing Young Bizzy, the head of the cocaine squad that just fucked him over with a bad package, made his blood boil. As Young Bizzy drove pass, Gusto looked at Chameleon and noticed the awkward look on her face.

"What, you know that nigga or something?", he asked in a hostile manner. "No I don't know his corny looking ass." Gusto stared deep into her eyes, trying to sense if she was lying or not, but he couldn't read her. "Lets go in the house", he stated. The both of them walked up the porch steps and went inside.

CHAPTER 7: WAIT FOR THE BLOW

It was 10:00 AM, and Geronimo was standing on the exact same corner he always did when waiting for Da'white to serve him his order. Gusto went over the plan over and over again to make sure Geronimo knew exactly what he had to do. The thought of it all had him extremely nervous. He really didn't want things to lead to this, he would rather call Da'white and settle things verbally. But when he saw how Gusto reacted, he decided not to express himself. "Man I hope everything go smooth", Geronimo thought to himself. He was looking at Gusto, who sat across the street inside the Georgie's Fried Chicken fast food restaurant. Gusto stared back at him through the huge glass window. While the customers were standing in line and putting in their food orders, Gusto sat eating at the wooden table by the window, trying to blend in.

Da'white's car finally turned up Trent Street. Gusto made a smooth move out of his seat, and out of the store. Butterflies began dancing around in Geronimo's stomach when he saw Gusto exit the fast food spot. "Calm down Geronimo, calm down", he said to himself trying to get his nerves under control. He began walking up the street to where Da'white parked his car. As Geronimo moved towards the passenger side of the car, Gusto rushed towards the car from across the street holding his shiny chrome 357 Magnum. Geronimo opened both the passenger and the back door at the same time. Gusto rushed in. "Move and I'm going to blow your fucking head off!", he growled as he climbed in the backseat, holding the gun to the back of Da'white's head. Da'white threw his hands in the air. "Oh word, this how y'all doing y'alls", Da'white stated as he looked at Geronimo from the corner of his eye. He tried his best to calm his nerves in order to not show any signs of fear. "Shut the fuck up!", Gusto demanded. Geronimo leaned down and grabbed the bag with the work from underneath the driver seat. "I got it." Da'white noticed Geronimo's uneasiness and smirked. "I hope y'all niggas ready for what's about to come y'all way after this." BOOM! Gusto had zero tolerance for tuff guys and bold threats, so he pulled the trigger and sent a huge slug through the back of Da'white's head. His brains splattered all over the front windshield and dashboard, as his lifeless body fell forward over the steering wheel, causing the horn to sound off loudly.

Geronimo's ears were ringing from the loud sound of the shot fired. Seeing a man bleeding profusely from a hole that was blasted in his head was just too much for Geronimo. He lost it. "Aaaaghhh!", he screamed to the top of his lungs hysterically like a straight up bitch. He dropped the bag of coke, got out of the car, and began running as fast he could down the street. He was so shook he didn't even realize he was running in the opposite direction from where the getaway car was waiting. Gusto's jaw dropped. "What the fuck type shit this nigga on", he thought to himself. He began surveying the area making sure no one witnessed what just went down. He stuffed his gun in his pocket and leaned forward to grab the coke from out of the passenger seat. He then calmly got out the car, and began speed walking towards the getaway car around the corner, driving straight to the trap house. He hoped to see Geronimo along the way, but didn't.

As soon as Gusto opened the front door, he saw Geronimo leaned forward on the couch with his elbows resting on his knees breathing extremely heavy. He had beat Gusto to the house by a few seconds. "There your bitch ass go", Gusto was still disappointed in his partner. He used his foot to slam the door shut and tossed the gym bag on the couch. Gusto was so upset with Geronimo for running off and leaving him behind knowing he only had one hand. He was pondering whether he should kill him or not. "Why the fuck you drop the shit and run off like that!" Gusto pointed

42

his finger in Geronimo's face while standing over top of him. Still struggling to catch his breath, Geronimo raised his index finger indicating he needed a minute. He finally said, "Because you killed the nigga, that's why I ran off. That wasn't part of the plan, you did some bullshit." "What the fuck you mean I did some bullshit!", Gusto snapped. "Ol boy got on some tuff guy shit so he got what he deserved. Fuck was I supposed to do." Not knowing what to say, Geronimo just shook his head. "So what are we going to do now?" Gusto looked at him like he was crazy. "What the fuck you caught amnesia or something? We gonna sell all the coke, split half the money up,and then go spend the other half with Butchy!" "Man alright, I guess", Geronimo replied still sounding worried.

The pathetic look on Geronimo's face let Gusto know he wasn't ready to take things to the next level, but it was definitely too late in the game to be turning back. It was either kill Geronimo and keep all the coke for himself, or let him live off the strength of them being close friends. He would just have to make sure Geronimo stayed only in the hustling side of things. "Man this bitch ass nigga lucky he my nigga or else I would have blew his fucking head off too", Gusto thought to himself, hoping he would never regret the decision he just made. "Listen man, now ain't the time to be pussyfooting around. We just took it to the next level! It's either all, or nothing at all. You hear me?" Geronimo nodded his head in agreement. "Yeah I got you bro, I was tripping when that shit went down, my fault." "Shit, they don't call me Gusto for nothing. Now lets go cook this coke up and get this money!"

CHAPTER 8: *"You get another shot."*

Gusto cruised down Brunswick Avenue in a black Cadillac. He was on his way to pick up Tayla and take her on their first date. He pulled up and parked in front of a brown and green house. When he didn't see Tayla on the porch waiting for him, he though he arrived too early. He pulled out his cell phone and saw that it was 6:30. "Oh I'm right on time", he stated before beeping the horn. Several seconds later, Tayla came walking out the front door. Her fresh pair of pink and white Air Max's matched her pink Polo v-neck short sleeve shirt, which fit her upper fame perfectly, making her perky breast appear as if they were going to burst out of her shirt. Her grey Polo sweatpants wasn't too tight, but her voluptious thighs and bubble butt was still on display. As she leisurely strolled to the car, Gusto licked his lips while his lustful eyes watched her every step. "Damn she sexy as hell", he thought to himself in admiration.

Once Tayla climbed in the car, she smiled at her date. "Hey Gusto." "What's up baby." Tayla looked at the cast on Gusto's arm, it must have slipped her mind that he was injured with only one capable hand. "Umm umm boy, you can't be driving me around with your arm all messed up like that." "You don't have to worry. I got the wheel", he assured nonchalantly. "Nope, that's how people get in car accidents. I want to have a good time, not get hurt. Let me drive or we ain't going no where." Gusto just stared at her. She continued, "What? I got my license." "Alright, you can drive. Just don't run into any parked cars or houses", he stated jokingly before he got out to get in on the passenger side. While Tayla was putting her seat belt on and buckling up for safety, Gusto leaned his seat all the way back. "So where we going?", she asked placing her small hands on the large steering wheel. "Wherever you want to go." A surprised expression appeared on Tayla's face. "Anywhere I want to go huh." She began thinking of where she wanted to go. "Let's go to the bowling alley." Out of all the places in the city, a bowling alley was the last place Gusto expected to hear her say. "You wanna go to a whack ass bowling alley?", he thought to himself with a displeased look on his face. "What? Something wrong with the bowling alley?", Tayla noticed Gusto's expression. "Nah, ain't nothing wrong. Come on, let's go."

As soon as Gusto stepped inside the huge bowling alley he was amazed at how the crowds of people were acting like they were having the time of their life. He never been bowling before, but saw it on tv and always considered it a corny sport. "Take your shoes off and give them to the people at the counter", Tayla instructed. The two approached the huge counter that had many different shoe slots, and began taking off their sneakers. Gusto followed Tayla's lead. Three white women were standing behind the counter waiting to help. One of them came over to the couple. "May I help you?", the blonde hair white woman politely asked. "Yes, we're going to play two games", Tayla stated, placing their shoes on the counter. "That will be thirty dollars." Tayla started to go in her pocket for the money. Gusto looked at her and smirked. "Tayla if you don't knock it off. You don't ever have to pay for nothing when you with me." He thought it was cute that she tried to pay for the games. It also let him know she wasn't the type of girl that would try and chew though his pockets. Gusto handed the money to the lady behind the counter. Once she grabbed the couple's shoes, she placed them on the counter. "Here you go. You two will be playing on aisle 4 and 5." Gusto picked up his pair of bowling shoes. "What the hell kind of shoes is these, clown shoes?" Tayla and the woman behind the counter started giggling. "No they ain't no clown shoes boy. Just put them on." "This must be his first time bowling", the woman chimed in. "I know right. So you know I got to beat him while I teach him", Tayla said while looking at Gusto.

Tayla led Gusto to their bowling aisles. Gusto began surveying the bowling area. The wood floor was extremely shiny and there were twelve different bowling aisles with huge tv's mounted from the ceiling to keep score. Once they made it to their seats Tayla explained to Gusto how to pick the correct ball. "Alright, now make sure the ball you grab ain't too heavy. I don't want you hurting yourself." Tayla chose a pink bowling ball and Gusto chose a ball he felt comfortable to hold and swing down the lane. "Ok, it's showtime!" Tayla was excited to show off her skills. "Now listen, try your best to aim the ball straight down the middle of the lane, that way you have a better chance of knocking down all the pins. Watch me first." Tayla's father taught her how to bowl before he passed away several years ago. She stepped on to the shiny wooden floor, took a deep breath before cocking her hand back, and then rushed toward the center forcefully throwing her bowling ball straight down the lane. They both watched eagerly as the pink bowling ball crashed against the pins, knocking them all down. Tayla pumped her fist in the air as she turned to face Gusto. "Oh my gosh, I rolled a strike on the first shot. Now it's your turn."

Tayla's joyful attitude uplifted Gusto's spirit. She was totally different from all the other girls he was used to being with. Gusto picked up the bowling ball and made his way to the lane. He noticed an older white bald man beside him doing a funny dance after knocking down all his pins, causing a crowd of people to laugh uncontrollably. "If this goofy old man can roll a strike, I know I can",Gusto thought to himself. Gusto ran up and threw the ball as hard as he could, slightly loosing his balance. The bowling ball crashed against the pins, but he only knocked down five. "Damn", he stated in a low tone. When he turned around, he noticed a few people staring at his broken arm. "What the fuck, y'all

46

ain't never see a nigga with a broke arm before", he thought. Tayla broke his concentration, "Gusto you did good!" She was clapping and cheering, until she noticed the displeased look on his face. "Fix your face and go back up there and knock the rest of those pins down. You get another shot. Use my ball this time." Gusto looked down at the pink bowling ball and laughed saying, "I ain't using no pink bowling ball." Tayla started laughing too. "Ain't nothing wrong with pink." Once the machine spit Gusto's black ball out, he grabbed it and made his way back to the floor. He stood still, and lined his body up with the pins on the left. "Aight. Now it's time to make it happen. Go get the rest of those bitches for daddy", he mumbled before taking another stab at it. This time, he managed to knock down two more pins. "At least you knocked a few more down. The first time I went bowling, I missed all the pins my first couple of tries." "Yeah, it ain't about nothing. I'll knock'em all down next time." "Alright well, you stay here and practice on my side while I go grab us some food", she stated. Gusto reached to get some money from his pocket, but Tayla already rushed off to the other side of the bowling alley.

Once Tayla came back with the food and drinks, the two continued to bowl and get to know each other. Gusto became more comfortable with his date and began bowling strikes back to back. He was so in to the game, he went back to the counter and paid for a few more rounds. They were so caught up in the moment, they didn't realize the bowling alley was closing until the owners began turning off some of the lights. Gusto and Tayla left the bowling alley and made their way back to Tayla's house. Once in front, Tayla parked the car. "So, did you have fun?", she asked. Gusto looked at her and smiled. "You know I did." "Yeah, me too." The both of them locked eyes for a few seconds before she continued. "So what you about to go do, go home to your girlfriend?" Gusto raised his eyebrows, looking at her as if she said something wrong. "I ain't got no girlfriend." After

47

having the time of his life and learning so many good things about Tayla, he was willing to do whatever it took to make her his lady, except remove Chameleon completely out of his life. Since they were from two totally different worlds, he convinced himself that he could have both of them as his wifey and never get caught. "After I leave here, I'm going to handle some business." "Oh so you don't have one?", she asked again, hoping he wasn't lying. Gusto licked his full lips. "Nah, I'm trying to work on getting one though." "Right. So what you doing tomorrow?" "Whatever you doing", he said putting a smile on Tayla's face. "Alright then, I'll call you tomorrow around five o'clock." "Ok, let me walk you to your door." The both of them got out the car, walked to the porch, and then turned to face each other. "Alright, make sure you get home safe", she stated sensing that he wanted a kiss. "Don't worry, I will", he stated while grinning. Tayla perked up, locking eyes with Gusto. Gusto leaned in closer with his head tilted to the side, maintaining eye contact. And then... The front door swung open with Tayla's mother standing in the doorway. "Girl what you out there doing?". Tayla was caught off guard, and gasped while she turned to face her mother. "Nothing mom. Just telling my friend good night." "Your friend?" Tayla's mom was curious to see who this friend was. "How you doing? How about y'all step inside." She wanted to get a better look at him. Tayla and Gusto stepped inside. "How you doing miss, my name is Germain." Looking him up and down, she sensed he was a thug. "So where are you and my daughter coming from this time of night?" "We just came from the bowling alley. We was there all day." Just then, Tayla's brother Kevin came walking out the kitchen, holding a can of grape soda. "What's up sis. Where you was at all day?" He stopped in his tracks when he noticed the male stranger in the living room. "I was out bowling with my friend", she replied. Kevin walked up on Gusto and introduced himself. "What's good, I'm Kevin." "My name

48

Germain", Gusto replied still going with his birth name. The two slapped hands. Kevin just shook his head, as he walked back into the kitchen. Tayla's mother continued to question her daughter's new friend, and Gusto had all the answers. After a while, he went on his way. Tayla's mother warned her daughter that Gusto was a thug, and she made it clear that she never wanted to see him step foot anywhere near her house again. Despite her mother's warning, Tayla could not resist the strong attraction she had towards Gusto and the two continued to see each other.

CHAPTER 9: STAY SCHEMING

It was 85 degrees outside, and Gusto was sitting on Shaky's porch steps with a pint of cognac in between his legs. He was waiting for Chameleon to come back with some headache medicine. He just found out from his cousin Butchy that shit was dry, and he was no longer the man to see for weight. "Damn man, what the fuck I'm gonna do now", he thought. He started to realize that killing Da'white might have been a big mistake. Gusto knew he had to come up with a plan real quick. For one, his workers were almost done with the last of the coke and two, he knew if he stayed without product for too long his clientele would go else where.

Gusto picked up the bottle of cognac and took a huge gulp. He grunted as the burning sensation traveled through his chest. He looked up to see Chameleon and Geronimo walking down the street. "There her ass go", he said to himself. Shaky walked outside and grabbed a seat in one of the plastic chairs on the porch. Chameleon and Geronimo finally reached the house. "Did you get it?" "Yeah I got it. What you thought I forgot?", Chameleon stated with an attitude. She pulled out a bottle of pain killers from a small brown paper bag. "Ya ass should have never took your cast off." She walked up the steps, brushing her big booty up against him, taking a seat next to Shaky. Chameleon was pissed with Gusto for taking the cast off a week earlier than he was supposed to. Gusto turned to look at her, "What you mean, I was still taking the medicine with it on. My arm good, see." He started bending and flexing his arm. Chameleon just rolled her eyes. "Boy just leave me alone. I don't feel like talking to you right now." Knowing how she was, Gusto decided to leave her be.

Geronimo looked at Shaky, threw both of his hands in the air, and spread them wide. "There goes my baby", he sang as he began dancing to his own rhythm doing a two step. Shaky burst into laughter, shaking her head from side to side. "Boy you so stupid." "Yes he is girl", Chameleon chimed in. Shaky knew Geronimo was real big on her, but she would never give him the time of day. She saw him as the fake and fronting type. "Huh girl, role up." Chameleon grabbed a strawberry blunt wrap from out her bag and handed it to Shaky. "A yo", Gusto said grabbing Geronimo's attention. Geronimo took his eyes off Shaky to look at Gusto. "What's good bro." "What's going on down the street?", Gusto asked. "Nothing really. Hook Dog and Itty Bitty in the alley doing what they do, and a few young boys was on the corner selling weed." Geronimo looked at Chameleon and chuckled. "Until your girl cursed them out and made them get off the corner." "You mu'fucking right, them little dirty ass young boys was trying to cut our weed money off", Chameleon stated in a high tone before taking a sip from the flavored water bottle she held in her hand. Even though she was sexy as hell, she put the G in ghetto and was ready to throw down with anyone at any given moment. Shit, she even tried Gusto's chin sometimes. Geronimo got back to his conversation with Gusto. "Oh yeah, I seen papi go in to the store wearing a book bag, dressed like he just came from school or something." Gusto looked away for a few seconds, taking in what Geronimo just said. "Lango just walked in the store?", Gusto stated in an eager tone. "Yeah", Geronimo replied, wondering why Gusto became so excited all of a sudden. A cunning idea popped in Gusto's head. He remembered Lango sold heavy amounts of cocaine on the low, and only dressed like that when he was about to go handle business. Lango would also meet up and do transactions with a few of his Latin brothers on the next block over. "Wait here, I'll be right back", Gusto stated before he got up from the steps. He rushed to his car and sped up the street.

Gusto called Lil Petey and Chopo to meet up, once they were together they headed towards Sweets Avenue, the place where he always saw Lango making his deals. Gusto already knew Lango didn't like him too much, and therefore would never do any illegal business with him, so he desperately hoped the tactical scheme he quickly put together would work. The two young gangsters, Lil Petie and Chopo, were both masked up. "Listen y'all, just rob him. He's dressed like he going to school and he got a book bag on. You understand?" Gusto explained carefully as he looked back at the two. They both nodded their head in agreement. Gusto looked around to survey the area. "Go wait on the side of the those two houses. Soon as he walk pass, grab him and whack him." The two young soldiers climbed out the car, ran in between the two houses, and hid behind two large garbage cans. Gusto drove off and stopped at the corner of Sweets Avenue and the Boulevard, he looked through his rear view mirror and spotted Lango making his way out of the alley. A wicked grin spread across Gusto's face as he made the left turn down the Boulevard.

Lango whistled as he walked up Sweets Avenue, holding his hands in his pockets. He was short and skinny, and rocked a curly mini afro. He was in his mid thirties, but his bare face made him look like he was in his early twenties. "Damn man, where the hell Poncho at", he thought to himself. He pulled his left hand out of his pocket, and checked his gold Rolex for the time. It was 4:28, which meant he was two minutes early. "He should be turning down Sweets any minute now." Suddenly, Lango felt someone grab him by his shirt. He was forcefully snatched in between the two houses. "What the fuck…" Before Lango could finish the last word, Lil Petey smacked him with the butt of his gun. "Ugghh!", Lango groaned in pain as his head began to ache. "Now shut the fuck up!", Lil Petey growled, pointing the gun to Lango's head. He still had him gripped up by his shirt. "Take the book bag from him." Chopo took the bag from Lango, and put it on his back. "Lay flat on your stomach, and count to a thousand", Lil Petey ordered. Lango, was shaking uncontrollably. He placed his hands on his head, laid on the dirty ground, and began counting out loud. Chopo and Lil Petey ran as fast as they could.

Lango was so afraid that he counted all the way up to five hundred. When he finally realized he was all alone, he got up from off the ground. He began to dust himself off, rubbing the swollen lump on his head. Lango quickly made his way back to the store. Once he made it to the boulevard, he saw Gusto standing near the bodega on the corner watching a crowd of young boys rolling dice in front of an abandoned house. When Lango got closer he grunted in pain, "Awe man, my fucking head is killing me." Gusto looked at Lango with a shocked expression on his face. "What happened man, you alright?" "Nah, I ain't alright. Some fucking stick-up kids just robbed me for two keys", he admitted angrily, still rubbing the knot on his head. Gusto wanted to laugh, but instead he twisted his face up to make it seem like he was upset. "Somebody just robbed you? Where at?" "Right on Sweets, just a few minutes ago." "Listen Lango, I know I don't kick it with you like how I do with all the other papi's in the store, but you they peoples so you my peoples." Gusto paused, waiting for Lango's response, but Lango kept quiet, so Gusto continued. "This my hood, and don't nothing go on around here unless I give the O.K., so I look at this shit as being disrespectful to me. Don't even trip though, I'm about to go try to find out who was behind this bullshit." Gusto said, looking Lango right in the eye. Lango felt a little relieved to know he had Gusto's support. "O.K. papi, I appreciate that." Gusto looked across the street at the crowd of young boys gambling and said, "Matter fact, hold up." He stormed across the street and ran up on the young men. Gusto snatched the red dice from off the ground, and threw them across the street as hard as he could. Then took his position in the middle of the crowd.

"Listen man, one of the papi's in the corner store just got pistol whipped and robbed on Sweets Ave. I better find out who was behind that bullshit before the day over with, or it's going to be a mu'fucking problem!" Gusto made sure to come across real aggressive with his message, making sure he said it loud enough for Lango to hear. A short chubby young man spoke up for everyone saying, "Man, we was right here gambling the whole time. We ain't have nothing to do with that shit." "That don't mean you don't know who did it", Gusto barked back, towering over the young boy. "Like I said, I better have some answers before the day over with!" Gusto walked back across the street where Lango stood watching his Oscar award winning performance. "I'll try my best not to put your business out there while I hunt down who did it", Gusto reassured him before walking to his car.

CHAPTER 10: WHO KILLED DA'WHITE

Meanwhile, the weed money flow just picked up. Shaky and Chameleon sat on the porch gossiping about everything going on around the neighborhood while serving their customers. "For real girl, he smacked her down to the ground outside in front of everybody", Chameleon stated in shock with her eye brows raised. "That's why she ain't been outside for the last couple days", Shaky told her. "Umm, well that couldn't have been me. We would've been brawling toe to toe, fuck that." Geronimo sat on the steps waiting for Gusto, listening to their conversation. "These bitches is crazy", he thought. He noticed a tall light skin man wearing a pair of blue jeans and a white t shirt walking towards him. "What's good Geronimo", the young man greeted. "What up bro", Geromino replied as he moved to the side, allowing him to walk up the steps. The young man, who was there to purchase a couple bags of haze, tried to push up on Shaky. "Umm, look at you Shaky. Pretty feet all out, smooth skin all oiled up", he stated while licking his lips. He gazed over her shiny legs and white open toe sandals while he stood over top of her. "You like what you see huh", she flirted back. Geronimo stood up and turned to face everyone on the porch. "Hold the hell up dog, that's wifey right there. Cop your weed and keep it moving." Shaky never entertained Geronimo when he showed interest in her, so for her to sit in his face and flirt with someone else caused him to become jealous. The young man turned around, holding up his hands. "Oh that's my fault. I didn't mean no disrespect." Shaky sucked her teeth. "Boy you ain't my man." Chameleon began laughing, "That boy crazy." The young man copped his weed and left. "Don't be doing that bullshit in front of me Shaky. You know I'm in love with you." Even though Geronimo was serious, he still managed to keep everyone laughing.

Geronimo was still facing Shaky when a gray Taurus with dark tents pulled up and parked a few houses down. Two men hopped out and began walking towards him. Geronimo finally turned around and was shocked to see the two young thugs coming his way. His heart started pumping. He recognized them right away, it was Bugsy The Bulldog and Ratchet Rob. They were two of the most vicious goons under Young Bizzy's organization. The both of them wore *R.I.P. Da'white* t-shirts. They were in the stash house with Da'white right before he went to serve Geronimo the two keys of coke, and was almost certain Geronimo had something to do with his death. "Geronimo, what's good boy", Bugsy stated in a menacing tone. He was a tall, skinny, brown skin rough looking man with a bald head. Bugsy pulled out a black 45 caliber hand gun from off his hip and barked, "What the fuck happened with Da'white!" Geronimo swallowed hard, he was so scared that he could barely talk. "I…I don't…I don't know what happened with him. Why you asking me?", he stated fumbling his words. Ratchet Rob noticed the two females sitting on the porch looking at them. "Don't do it, two bitches is on the porch", he warned. "Nah fuck that, something got to give", Bugsy said with clinched teeth. Thinking Geronimo was about to get killed, Shaky and Chameleon quickly hopped up from their seats and rushed inside the house, slamming the door shut.

Geronimo tried to stand up, but was met with a violent blow from the butt of Bugsy's gun. "Aggh!", Geronimo yelled as his head split open. Blood began to pour. Geronimo was about to fall to the ground but Bugsy caught him by his long braids, snatching and yanking his head back. He let off several shots in the air. BLOW! BLOW! BLOW! BLOW! Bugsy stuffed the extremely hot barrel all the way down Geronimo's throat, causing Geronimo to gag, slobber, and damn near choke to death. A muffled scream escaped Geronimo's mouth as the stinging

56

hot sensation started to consume him. "Listen you little bitch ass nigga…", Bugsy looked right in to his victim's watery eyes. "I know your man Gusto was the one that killed White Boy because your bitch ass ain't got the heart to do no shit like that. So tell him Bugsy the Bulldog was out here looking for him." Before he released the gun from his mouth, Bugsy looked at Ratchet Rob and said, "Take everything in his pockets." Ratchet Rob found five grand in each of Geronimo's front pockets, which he then stuffed into his. Bugsy finally took the gun out of Geronimo's bloody mouth and released his braids, causing him to fall to the ground gasping for air. The two thugs jumped back in their car and sped off. Shaky and Chameleon watched everything from the living room window. They immediately opened the front door and came to Geronimo's aid. They tried to call Gusto, but their calls went straight to voicemail.

CHAPTER 11: THE GIFT BEARER

Gusto already met up with his young soldiers to grab the coke they robbed Lango for, and was now on his way to the store to give back the stolen goods. He made sure to wait so it could seem like he spent all his time finding out who was responsible for the stick up. When Gusto pulled up in front of the deli, he noticed a few young men from the area standing on the corner. With the book bag strapped to his back, he made his way into the store. The melodic sound of Latino music was playing throughout the store. Talie, Lango's brother, was standing behind the counter, while three unfamiliar Spanish men stood in the back of the store where they served food. "Gusto! Como esta papi!", he greeted cheerfully. Talie was a lean Puerto Rican man with thick dark wavy hair and a full beard. He was a cool type of guy who always made his store customers feel warm and welcome. This was especially true for Gusto, the neighborhood top dog who in exchange made sure no one ever gave him any problems. Talie even tried talking his little brother Lango in to supplying Gusto with cocaine a while back, but Lango refused. "What's good Talie", Gusto replied with a half smile, as he approached the counter and slapped hands. "I got back what was taken from your brother." Talie's eyes grew wide. "Oh shit, you really got it back." Lango already told his brother what went down earlier. And even though the two brothers appreciated the gesture, they both doubted that Gusto would get the cocaine back. "Alright then, follow me." Talie began walking towards the back of the store with Gusto following behind him. Once they made it to the back Talie said something in Spanish to the other men, which made them turn to look at Gusto. Talie continued through a door which led to a small hallway, eventually stopping at another door which led to the basement.

Lango was seated on a long tiger stripe couch with his eyes shut and head tilted back. There was a matching rug on the floor with a slim Spanish female on her knees sucking his dick like her life depended on it. After taking a loss, he decided to have one of his sex buddies come over and help him take his mind off of things. "A yo Lango", Talie smirked as him and Gusto stood side by side a few feet away. Lango jumped as his eyes popped open. Feeling embarrassed, the pretty Spanish woman quickly got up off her knees allowing Lango to tuck his erect penis back in to his pants. "Aww man y'all crept up on me", Lango stated. "We ain't creep up on you. You had your eyes closed", Talie responded, still finding his little brother amusing. The young female sat on the couch in silence, trying to avoid eye contact with the other two men. Gusto took off the book bag, and tossed it to Lango. "Look inside and tell me if that's everything that was taken from you." Lango unzipped the bag to check, and suddenly a huge smile appeared on his face. He was speechless. "I told you he was good people, and could be trusted", Talie stated. Lango had no choice but to agree with his brother, Gusto just saved his ass a whole lot of money. "Yeah I guess you were right all along." Lango relaxed back in his seat and said, "So Gusto, how much you usually pay for one of these?" He then pulled out one of the keys of coke that was wrapped in plastic. "To keep it real with you, it's been so long since I bought one, I nearly forgot. I usually get three at a time at 15 stacks a piece", Gusto lied trying to see what level they were on in the game. "Oh is that right? From watching the way you and your friend hustle, I thought y'all was already that heavy." "Well that goes to show you, looks can be deceiving", Gusto started grinning. Lango began laughing, "Yeah you right, because y'all damn sure fooled the hell out of me." Talie started laughing too. Slowly, a serious expression appeared on Lango's face. "But listen, I can't get you more than three keys at a time." Gusto shot him a look as if to say "Damn that's all you working with." Lango continued, "But I can get you as much dope you want, for a very cheap price and real good too." Gusto laughed to himself knowing that not only did his tactic work, but it also opened up another door. Gusto sold dope before, and knew that the money was good, but it made him very hot with the police so he left it alone. "How cheap?", he asked. "A hundred dollars for each pack, as long as you buying over two hundred and fifty of them." "Damn, only a hundred dollars", he thought to himself. "Alright, so when we gonna get this shit started." "You going to have to wait a week or two for the dope. I got to contact my family out of town first and let them know about you", Lango explained. "Alright so what's up with the coke? I need some as soon as possible." "Oh you can buy this coke off me right now. I already told my other buyer I got robbed for it." "Say no more, I'll be right back with the cash in no more than twenty minutes."

As soon as Gusto stepped out of the store, he spotted Shaky, Geronimo, and Chameleon standing across the street near his car. He could tell by the look on everyone's face that something was wrong. "Where the hell you been at? We been looking all over for you", Chameleon stated raising her voice as she approached him. "I was in the back of the store handling some important business", he explained. Chameleon stood in front of him with her hands on her hip. "I hope it was as important as you say cause while you was back there, two dudes robbed Geronimo in front of Shaky's house." Gusto looked at Geronimo and frowned. "Who was it?" Geronimo tried to talk, but Gusto couldn't understand him. The hot gun barrel that was shoved in his mouth left burns on his throat, tonsils, and tongue. "What the fuck wrong with him?", Gusto asked Shaky. "They shot the gun in the air before they put it in his mouth, he might have to go to the hospital. And I think they said something about Da'white, and that they looking for you", Shaky explained. "Word up, they said something about Da'white?" "Yeah, I heard he got killed a couple of days ago, what happened?", Chameleon asked being nosey. She knew Da'white was Bizzy's cousin. "I don't know?", Gusto stated. Chameleon sucked her teeth. "Well since you don't know, me and Shaky about to go back to the house and finish selling our weed." She looked at Shaky and said, "Let's go get this money girl." The two young women started walking up Fountain Avenue. "Come on Geronimo", Gusto stated as he got in to his car and sped off.

At first, Gusto thought it was the Haitians, but after hearing the name Da'white and how boldly the two wild goons came in his hood looking for him, he knew exactly who it was: Bugsy the Bulldog and Ratchet Rob! They were the only two goons that were apart of Young Bizzy's team that were brazen enough to pull a stunt like that. Gusto still had serious business to handle, so he went to grab the money from his house so he could pick up the coke from Lango. After dropping the coke off at the house, Geronimo and Gusto spent several hours driving around looking for Bugsy and Ratchet Rob. They drove down every single street in Trenton twice, but didn't see them any where so Gusto decided to fall back for the night. "Those bitch ass niggas ain't no where to be found. We mine as well go to the liquor store, grab a bottle of Henny, and go back to the trap", he stated as he drove down West State Street. He made a left on Hermitage Ave, and another left on Stuyvesant Avenue, pulling up in front of a liquor store. There was a group of young men standing a few feet away. "Go grab us a pint of Henny and a box of Black and Milds real quick." Gusto pulled two crispy twenty dollar bills from his pants pocket, and tried to hand it to Geronimo. Geronimo looked at him and pointed at his mouth. "Damn, I forgot that fast", Gusto stated. Suddenly, a blue mini van pulled up beside them slamming on the brakes causing the tires to screech loudly. The passenger side door was open. Gusto looked to his side and gasped when he saw a dark skin man with long dreads wave a black Mac 10 machine gun out the window. "Duck!", Gusto tried to warn before the man started spraying. BLAAAAAAT! BLAAAAAAT! BLAAAAAAT! The gunman let loose. Everyone standing in front of the store started running for dear life. "Stay down! Stay down!" Gusto was in a state of panic. The gunman continued squeezing as a hail of bullets bust through the car. Glass from the window shattered in to tiny pieces and fell all over the place. "Get out and make sure he's dead", the man driving the minivan ordered with a strong accent. "Oh shit, it's those fucking Haitians", Gusto thought to himself nervously while still ducked down in his seat. As soon as Gusto heard the man getting out the car, he put the car in drive, and pressed on the gas peddle as hard as he could. He was still ducking low in his seat, so he couldn't see what was in front of him. Gusto recklessly sped down the street, swerving from the sidewalk to the street. The gunman stood in the middle of the street with his gun drawn. BLAAAAAAT! BLAAAAAAT! BALLET! He was still letting off shots, hitting the back of Gusto's car. Once he made it far enough down the street, Gusto sat up to grab hold of the steering wheel, speeding away down the long street.

CHAPTER 12: FONZ

Young Bizzy drove down the busy street of Hamilton Avenue in his egg shell Mercedes Benz. Chameleon sat in the passenger seat staring at him. She was trying to figure out what to say to him. He hadn't spoke a word since he picked her up, and she knew exactly why. She just had to figure out a way to get him to tell her what was going on inside his head. "Damn baby, what's wrong? You look like you got something on your mind." "Ain't nothing wrong. I'm good", Bizzy gave a dry response. After finding out about his cousin's murder he was ruined and extremely cautious. He switched his cell phone number, and closed up shop for a while. Even though his top goons Bugsy and Ratchet Rob told him they were certain that Geronimo and Gusto were responsible for killing Da'white, he still felt suspicious about the whole situation. Knowing how greedy and slimy your own people could be when it came to the almighty dollar, he wouldn't be surprised if they had something to do with it. Bizzy was feeling confused and somewhat afraid, not knowing who to trust. Chameleon sucked her teeth, "Boy who you think you fooling. I know when something wrong with you." Bizzy began to wonder whether or not to talk about the situation. Gusto was her man, so he was hesitant to express himself, but at the same time Chameleon had Bizzy under the impression that she would leave Gusto at the drop of a dime. Shit, he figured she would be more loyal to him than anything. "I don't feel like it", he told her. Chameleon quickly snatched her hand from off his stomach. "What you don't trust me or something?", she stated with an attitude. "Fuck it, maybe she could put me on if them niggas really are behind this shit", he thought, finally giving in. "Yeah I trust you bae." The car stopped at a red light, and Bizzy turned to face Chameleon. "Then why you acting all uncomfortable and shit", she asked. "Because it's a whole lot of shit going on, and I have to be on point", he explained. "What's going on and why you have to be on point", she asked. Bizzy hung his head low and took a deep sigh before looking back at Chameleon. "My cousin was robbed and killed a few days ago." Chameleon mouth fell open, "Who, Da'white!" Bizzy nodded his head and said, "Yeah." The traffic light turned green, as Bizzy pulled off, a black pick up truck slowly drove in front of him. "Oh my gosh, I'm so sorry to hear that", she stated. "Yeah I was too." "Who was it and what did they rob him for?" "He was robbed for two keys and word is that your people did it", he told her looking to see her reaction. "My peoples who!", she exclaimed in a curious tone. "Gusto and his man Geronimo." Chameleon didn't say a word, but the facial expression spoke *are you serious*. "That's crazy, because if that's the case those niggas should have a whole lot of coke and money. But it seem like they dealing with the same shit." "Yeah, just because that's the way it seem don't mean that's the way it is. Listen baby, I really need you to find out how much work those niggas really holding. My cousin already told me that they don't never buy no more than one key of coke." "Alright baby, I'll do that for you and it won't be a problem neither. I know where he stash all his money and coke at." She reached her hand out and began gently rubbing his manhood. Bizzy's penis hardened as his body tensed up. A naughty grin appeared on Chameleon's face, as she licked her juicy pink lips. "Now let me help take your mind off things for a little while." She unzipped his pants and began sucking his dick while he cruised the Wilber Section area of Trenton.

Chameleon was lying her ass off when she told Bizzy she would let him know if Gusto had an unusual amount of money. The last thing she wanted them to do was go to war with each other and end up in jail. That meant she would no longer reap the benefits of having two cash cows, who would grant her whatever amount of milk she requested. After sucking the life out of Young Bizzy, and getting a few dollars from him, Chameleon had him drop her off on East State Street in front of a clinic. She told him she was going to get a check-up, which was also a lie. She was really meeting up with some guy named Fonz she met when he came to buy weed a couple weeks ago. She heard his name ringing in the streets as a notorious stick up kid that robbed all the big time drug dealers. She saw him as a potential way to get money from a different side of town. "Where the hell he at?", Chameleon said to herself impatiently as she looked up and down the street. "Fuck this, I'm about to call Shaky to pick me up." She took her cell phone out of her Prada purse, and began walking down the street. Within seconds, she spotted Fonz's black tented out Intrepid coming her way. "Oh there he go." As soon as Fonz pulled up on the side of her she got inside the car. "Damn baby, I thought you forgot about me for a minute." "Nah, it ain't like that, I'm just a little late because I'm in the process of doing my pick ups", the brown skin young man with box braids stated. He waited for a green Mustang to drive past him and then pulled off behind it. "I know you wouldn't do me like that. I'm just joking." Chameleon let out a fake laugh, intrigued to hear he was picking up. "I only gotta go to one more spot to pick my paper up, and then we could go out and grab something to eat." "Fine with me." Chameleon began snapping her fingers to the rhythm of the Kanye West song that played in the car. "I ain't saying she a gold digger, but she ain't messing with no broke nigga. Get down girl get down. This my song!" She turned the volume up and sang every word. Fonz chuckled and shook his head while turning on to Chambers Street, driving over the bridge heading towards his destination. Fonz finally made it to the Roger Gardens Housing Project. He slowly drove down Eisenhower where he noticed Reese(the person he was coming to visit) car parked in front of the three story building. Fonz turned the corner and parked near a black gate. "I'll be back in less than five minutes." He left out, leaving the car running. Chameleon watched him walk down the street until he disappeared around the corner. "Umm he walk like he got a big dick." She dug in her purse, pulled out a bag of weed and a blunt wrap, and began rolling up.

Meanwhile, Fonz just stepped inside the pissy hallway of the building, and walked up the first flight of stairs. He came to an apartment door and began knocking. KNOCK! KNOCK! KNOCK! "Who is it!", a male voice yelled from behind the door. A devious grin appeared on Fonz's face as he looked down using the brim of his black baseball cap to block his face out the peephole. Reese, a tall dark skin man with huge pink lips, sat on the black suede couch in the living room next to his friend A.B. A huge zip lock bag filled with purple haze was on his lap and a black bag filled with money sat on the floor near his feet. "Bro, unlock the door", Reese demanded. A.B. stood up and unlocked the door. Fonz forcefully pushed the door open and quickly stepped inside the apartment with his chrome 40 caliber hand gun pointed at A.B.'s head. "Get the fuck on the ground!" A.B. was speechless, and quickly did what he was told. "Oh shit!", Reese exclaimed as he put his hands up. He knew exactly who Fonz was and what he was about, he wasn't worried about getting robbed, he was worried about getting killed. "Please man don't..." Before he could finish his sentence Fonz yelled aggressively, "Shut the fuck up and don't move." "Reese, what's all that commotion going on in the living room?", Reese's mother yelled from her bedroom. She was laid up in her bed watching tv. "Awe man mom, please don't come out here", he thought to himself. Hearing someone else in the house, Fonz got on point. "I know you hear me boy." Reese's mother climbed out of her bed, slipped her feet in her blue slippers, and exited her bedroom. As soon as she stepped foot in the living room she saw a wild looking Fonz with his gun pointed at her. She jumped in shock and put her hands on

66

her chest. "Get the fuck on the ground!" After she laid on the ground, Fonz looked at Reese. "Who else here!" Scared to death, Reese began quickly shaking his head. "Nobody man, nobody." Fonz smirked at how scared he was. He spotted the large amount of weed on the couch. "Where the money at!" "It's...it's in...it's in the book bag", Reese stuttered. "Open it up and let me see. Hurry up." Reese picked the bag up from the floor, opened it, and held it up so Fonz could see inside it. Fonz looked down and saw the large amount of money. "Alright now put the weed in the book bag and hand it to me." Reese did exactly that. "Alright, now lay on the ground with everybody else", Fonz ordered as he stepped backwards out of the apartment.

Chameleon saw Fonz turn the corner with a bag in his hand. Once he got in the car, he tossed the bag in the backseat. Chameleon passed him the blunt of weed she was smoking on. "It took you kind of long." "I had to make sure everything was right. My bad." He took a pull off the blunt and went on like nothing ever happened.

CHAPTER 13: CHAMPAGNE AND ROOM KEYS

For the next several days, Gusto and Tayla picked certain times of the day to meet up with one another. Whenever they went out, they always had fun with each other. This particular day, they went to a New York City museum and ate dinner at an expensive restaurant afterwards. They were having so much fun, they decided to stay the night at one of the city's five star hotels. Tayla had Gusto doing things he would have never done and made him feel ways he had never felt. The most surprising thing about it all was that he embraced it and loved every minute. Normally, it only took a day or two for him to slide in between the legs of the average chick from the hood. This was usually based on his reputation or a smoke out and a bottle of liquor. Not with Tayla, she made him want it and work hard for it. She was able to keep him intrigued with her colorful personality and outgoing attitude. She was the first female he hung out with and didn't care whether or not they had sex. "Oh my gosh, let me find out this wrong key", Tayla stated giggling. She was feeling tipsy from the champagne they were drinking at the restaurant. Gusto was standing right up on her. "Let me see", he said smiling. "Oh, here it go." She finally got the door open. The two stepped inside the luxurious hotel suite. Gusto locked the door behind him while Tayla kicked off her shoes and strolled to the bathroom, leaving the door halfway open. Gusto took off his all white air forces, and grabbed the remote off the tv stand. He sat on the king size bed and flicked through the channels. Once he heard the shower water turn on a wide grin spread across his face, he knew exactly what time it was. "Umm. I'm going to tear her ass up. Finally!", he thought to himself anxiously.

When the shower stopped Tayla came strutting out of the bathroom completely nude and still soak and wet. Gusto immediately turned to look at her. His lustful eyes surveyed every single curve on her glistening body as she made her way across the spacious room until she stopped and stood directly in front of him. Her perky breast sat up high, her stomach was toned, and her waist was so small you could wrap both of your hands around it and feel your fingers touch. You could also see the structure of her heart shaped butt sitting up high from the front. Tayla noticed the amazed look on Gusto's face and smiled. "You like what you see?" She allowed him to stare a few seconds more, then she stated "So you just going to sit there?" Without saying a word, Gusto stood up and stuck his tongue in her mouth. Gusto kissed Tayla passionately while he gently placed his hand on the back of her head. Tayla matched his kisses with the same momentum, all while unbuckling his pants. Gusto's pants and boxers fell to the floor, and Tayla began massaging his erect penis. The thickness of his rod shocked her, she began thinking of how it would fill her insides. The thought of it made her juices overflow, trickling down her inner thigh. Gusto began licking and sucking on her neck, slowly working his way down to her mid-section. "Mmmmm", Tayla moaned as she closed her eyes and tilted her head back. Her small hands rubbed his broad shoulders and wide back as his thick tongue twirled around her hard nipples, then down her stomach, causing a tingling sensation to shoot up her spine.

Gusto dropped down to his knees, making sure he licked every single drop of water down to her ankles. Once he was done, he stood up and palmed her voluptuous ass with one hand and squeezed it, his fingers sank into her softness. They were standing so close to each other. "Get on the bed and lay on your stomach", he demanded in a low tone. Tayla did what she was told. Gusto took of his shirt and threw it to the floor before climbing in the bed. He was now over top of Tayla. He began to slowly lick her back, causing Tayla's body to squirm. "Oh my gosh", she moaned as her lip quivered. His warm tongue worked it's magic and drove her wild. She reached to grab a hold of the silk sheets in effort to control the nut she felt coming. It was no use, she came instantly. Gusto worked his way down to her heart shaped ass and began kissing it softly. The way Gusto's lips and tongue communicated with her soft body was something she never experienced before. Enough was enough! The vicious four play Gusto put down on her had her honey pot on fire, and it desperately needed to be put out by his extinguisher.

Gusto spread her ass cheeks and softly blew air in the crack of her ass. Tayla gasped for air. "What you trying to do to me", she said in a sexy tone. She glanced back at him and noticed the smirk on his face. "Give it to me Gusto." She turned around and laid on her back, spreading her legs wide open. "Let me lick it for a little bit first." "But I want to feel you inside of me." Tayla began rubbing on her soaking wet pussy. "Come on baby, give me that fat dick", she purred while licking her lips. Gusto was so turned on, he grabbed hold to her leg and placed it on her shoulder. He grabbed his long penis and slid it inside her wetness. "Sssss", she hissed when she felt his thickness penetrate her slit. Instantly her strong pussy muscles tightened. Feeling how tight she was Gusto carefully pushed as far inside her walls as they allowed, and began slowly stroking her, working his way in deeper and deeper. Staring deep in his eyes, Tayla bit down on her lip, placing her small hand on his muscular chest, caressing it. "Give it to me", she whispered in a pleading tone. Aroused by her soft touch and sexy voice, Gusto picked up his pace, taking deep powerful strokes. He placed both of his hands down on the mattress in a push-up position, going in and out, in and out, trying to find a rhythm. "Uhhhh", he grunted in pleasure, twisting his face up. Even though the feeling of Tayla's wetness was overwhelming, Gusto felt that he was too gangster to be moaning, so he tried his best to control himself.

Seeing all of Gusto's muscles flexing with every stroke he took, and the pleasant feeling of his rod digging into the deep depths of her ocean was too much for Tayla to bear at once. "Aaawww fuck me!", she screamed as she dug her nails into his broad chest. She wrapped her free leg tightly around his lower back. "Agghh", he growled loudly. A stinging sensation pierced his chest, which caused him to go into full blown beast mode. He began pounding her out so hard, the headboard banged against the wall. The gushy splash from Tayla's pussy could be heard with each powerful stroke he took. "Oooh Gusto", she screamed in ecstacy. She felt the tension of a powerful orgasm building up and Gusto felt it too, causing his mouth to fall open. He continued to beat it up. "I'm about to…" Before she could get the words out, her body began shaking uncontrollably. "Aaaaahhh", she moaned as she exploded all over his shaft. Gusto followed and exploded inside of Tayla. Both of their tangled body's went limp. Still breathing heavy, they stared deep into one another's eyes.

CHAPTER 14: LA CONEXION

The moment Gusto have been waiting for finally arrived. He sat in the back of a yellow taxi cab with a duffle bag of cash on his lap. The brown skin dread-head cab driver sped down the congested highway headed towards Paterson, New Jersey. Lango called him two days ago to let him know that everything was a go, and gave him the time, day, and location to meet up with the heroin connect. Gusto had already reached out to several dope dealers in the city to ask if they would consider doing business with him if he popped up with good product for a low price. All of their responses were yes. Gusto was eager to see how things would unfold. "My man, we almost there?", Gusto asked. The hip hop music that played over the radio was too loud, so the driver didn't hear him. "A yo!" Gusto tapped on the plastic partition. The driver turned the volume down. "What's up? How much longer do we have before we get there?", Gusto asked. "No more than ten minutes", the driver replied. Ten minutes later the driver slowly pulled up in front of a Spanish restaurant. A knot formed in Gusto's stomach and the palms of his hands began to sweat. This was going to be his first time dealing with the connect, so he didn't want to make any foolish mistakes, or give off a bad impression. "That'll be fifty dollars", the driver told him as he turned around to open the money slot. Gusto pulled a fifty dollar bill out of his pocket and stuffed it in the slot. "Thanks", he stated before clutching his duffel bag and climbing out of the vehicle. The taxi cab drove off, and Gusto made his way towards the restaurant entrance. He carefully observed his surroundings and noticed the neighborhood wasn't too bad of an area. All the houses on the street were nice with well kept lawns and clean sidewalks.

When he opened the door to step inside the restaurant, he saw that majority of the tables were occupied by Spanish patrons. Two beautiful female waitresses stood behind the counter a few feet away. "Damn where the hell I'm gonna sit", he thought as he looked around for an open table. Gusto never suspected that he was being watched by his new supplier's henchmen, who were blending in with the customers clocking his every move. "There go one right there." Gusto felt relieved after he spotted an open table on the far left side of the restaurant. One of the waitresses came from behind the counter and made her way over to him. "Hello sir, you must be our special guest", she greeted with a beautiful smile. Her silky jet black hair was put up in a huge stylish bun, and her facial features were very exotic. Lango took a picture of Gusto on his cell phone and sent it to the connect, so they already knew who he was. She noticed the lustful look in his eyes and chuckled. "Do you eat bistec y arroz?", she couldn't help mixing the two languages together. Gusto had no idea what bistec y arroz was, but he went along with it. "Yeah." "Ok, I'll be right back."

A few minutes later, she came back walking through the kitchen door holding two plates of food in her hand. She sat both plates of food down on the table. There was one plate with steak and onions in red sauce over rice, and the other plate held cooked bananas and a side salad with lettuce and tomatoes. "He'll be here any minute now", she assured him before turning around to go back behind the counter. Gusto kept his eyes on her for as long as he could, without looking too thirsty. "Umm, Umm. I'ma get me some of that", he mumbled under his breath. He wanted to push up on the beautiful waitress real bad but he didn't want to risk the chance of messing up the very profitable opportunity he cleverly created for himself. Instead, he made a mental note to wait and get established with the connect before making his move on her.

As Gusto began eating his food, he saw a casually dressed older man walk through the entrance door. He was tall and dark, with a full beard. "That must be then plug right there", he said to himself. Gusto began to admire the smooth looking Dominican boss, who wore a white and tan short sleeve button up shirt, flashing a gold Rolex watch on his wrist. "You don't mind if I sit here do you?", he asked with a heavy accent. "Nah, I don't mind." The man sat directly across from Gusto. "I'm Flocko", he introduced himself, stretching his hand across the table. Gusto made sure to give a firm handshake while he looked him dead in the eyes. "I'm Gusto." Flocko wasn't just a full blooded dope dealing veteran with enough smack to supply majority of the cities in New Jersey, he was also a very smart and legitimate business man who had zero tolerance for bullshit. Even though his cousin gave his word that Gusto was trustworthy and a certified hustler, Flocko wanted to meet him personally to fill him out before making any transactions. "Nice to meet you Gusto." Flocko got serious, making sure to maintain eye contact. "Now listen, once we're done talking and eating our food, you can go use the restroom on the other side of the restaurant. The third one is the only one that doesn't work. Understand?" "Yeah, I understand." A sly grin appeared on Flocko's face. "Alright then, lets get full." The waitress was just in time, bringing over Flocko's meal. "So tell me, how did you get the name Gusto?", he asked with a mouth full of food. "I got it from my die hard attitude and commitment to the hustle. To me it means all or nothing." "Oh yeah, that's what it means?" Flocko seemed somewhat impressed. "Sounds interesting. I can't wait to witness this for myself." "Oh you will." Just then, the waitress came over to refill their drinks. "Nina, what's up sexy woman", Flocko greeted her with a hint of excitement in his tone. Flocko was a married man, but he loved him some Nina. She was his mistress. "Hay papi, how you doing", she replied. Nina was a bit surprised to see him since he rarely came to the restaurant, let alone show his face when conducting illegal business. "You know me, just another day at the office", he said while gently rubbing her hand. "I bet it is", she stated smiling. "They must have fucked around or something", Gusto thought to himself as he analyzed how the two interacted with each other. "I don't give a fuck, I'm still going to get that pussy", he thought. "Your sister in the back, inside her office. Do you want me to tell her you're here?", Nina asked. "Nah, let her continue doing whatever it is she's back there doing", Flocko told her. Milli was Flocko's sister, and even though she was the owner of the restaurant, it was Flocko who ran the show. It was his money that started the business. "Okay, I'll let you two eat in peace. Have a good day." Nina turned around to assist a couple seated at the table near the entrance door. "She seem happy to see you", Gusto stated as he glanced at Flocko's wedding band. "Damn this nigga married and everythig. Shit, I don't blame him though. A bitch that bad, I'll cheat on my wife too", he thought. "Yeah, that's my favorite lady right there", he replied. Nina had been his side piece for years, but her mesmerizing presence always seem to have a strong effect on him, to the point where he would get overly excited whenever she would come around. For the next ten minutes Gusto and Flocko continued to converse over their meals. Once they were finished eating, they made their transaction and went on their way.

CHAPTER 15: YOUNG AND FLY

So many things changed during the past twelve months it was crazy! The extremely potent and low priced heroin provided by Flocko pushed the new team of young Trenton hustlers to the top. They had the town on smash and was touching more money than they could count. The common cars they used to drive turned in to foreign vehicles, gold chains and bracelets turned in to custom made platinum jewelry flooded with diamonds and other precious stones, the baddest broads were now their broads. To sum it all up they were stunting out of control, doing things they never imagined doing. Of course with all this winning came the haters. There were stick-up kids from every side of town scheming on their riches. Every time they turned around some one was putting a bug in their ear, telling them that such and such was going to do this and that. It didn't matter though, this new and successful team stayed on point. In fact, the haters helped to boost their ego. Their mentality was "fuck them hating ass niggas, let's stunt even harder!"

It was Spring time in the city of Trenton. The sun shined brightly in the clear blue sky, Gusto lived for days like this. The young hustler drove down Walnut Ave in his Pepsi blue Aston Martin convertible. His arm hung out the window allowing the sun-rays to hit the blue diamonds in his custom made bracelet. He was coming from the tattoo shop, and couldn't wait to show off the freshly greased up *Young Fly* tattoo that was etched in big and bold red letters across the top of his back. Gusto's shirt was off so he also got to show off his *Go Hard or Go Home* tattoo on his chest written in green ink with wads of hundred dollar bills falling down to his stomach. His light brown skin complexion showed the artistic literature vividly. The southern rapper Jeezy's lyrics blared through the car speakers as Gusto cruised down the street nodding his head to the beat. Everyone on the block turned to stare at the young baller in admiration. Gusto felt his cell phone vibrating. "Oh shit, somebody calling me", he said to himself. He quickly turned the music volume down to answer the call. "What up though", he answered, stopping the car on the corner of Walnut ave and Chambers street. "What's good nef? Where you been at?", the voice on the other end responded. Immediately Gusto recognized Geronimo's voice. "I was at the tattoo shop getting marked up. Why, what's good?" "We about to throw a small cookout in front of Shaky's house. I need you to grab a few blunts and a couple bottles of Remy", Geronimo stated. Gusto glanced across the street. "Alright, I'll grab it. I'm in front of the liquor store right now. Give me like five minutes." Gusto hung up from the call, and tossed the cell phone on the passenger seat. The block was full of young women and young thugs. Gusto noticed an older man yelling at a group of young boys standing in front of the liquor store. He was too far away to understand exactly what the man was saying. Before getting out, Gusto reached under his seat to get his black 40 caliber handgun. Even though his cousin Butchy was highly respected and grew up in the area, Gusto still made sure he was armed just in case some shit popped off. He was smart enough to know real live goons didn't give a fuck who your peoples were when it came to the cash. "I dare one of these niggas to try something."

All eyes were on him as he climbed out of his Aston Martin. As he got closer to the liquor store, the words of the older man became clearer. "Ain't none of these niggas out here fucking with me. I get that fucking cake!" The man was talking with his hands, boasting proudly to the group of young boys. "You see that Cadillac right there?" He waved his hand toward the silver Cadillac parked near the curb. "I just spent thirty thousand and drove off the lot with it." The man had his back turned, so he didn't see Gusto walking up from behind. "This clown ass nigga out here trying to talk that talk to these young boys that don't know no better." Gusto shook his head as he walked passed the man. The man was boasting about the same car he had when he was broke last year. As soon as Gusto walked inside the liquor store, he felt the cool breeze from the air conditioner hit his skin. "A yo papi, let me get a box of blunts and that ninety dollar bottle of Remy Martin", he stated as he approached the tall Puerto Rican man standing behind the counter. The man grabbed the expensive bottle of cognac while Gusto reached in his pocket and pulled out a wad of cash, placing two hundred dollar bills on the counter. The man handed Gusto the items in a plastic bag, and picked the money up. Before the man could open the register to give him his change and receipt, Gusto said, "Keep the change." He exited the store. Once back outside, he noticed the man was still running his mouth and bragging. "This piss head still out here talking about that bullshit ass car", he said to himself. "That's a nice car", Gusto complimented. In mid sentence, the older man stopped talking and looked at Gusto. Gusto also had the young boys full attention. "Oh you like the Cadi huh", the older man smiled. "I just spent like thirty stacks on this damn thing right here", he stated proudly. Gusto smirked. "Oh yeah, that's funny cause I just spent the same amount of paper on the diamonds in my bracelet", he stated sarcastically. Gusto motioned his hand wrist so everyone could see his bracelet, causing the diamonds to sparkle. All the young boys eyes grew wide in amazement. "Damn!", they all said in unison. Gusto walked off smoothly, while the older man turned and watched him. His envy towards Gusto grew even more when he saw him get in his foreign car. Gusto got in his ride, turned the music up, and pulled off.

Before going to Shaky's house, Gusto stopped at Talk Slick's spot to drop off some money. As soon as he stepped foot inside the house, the foul odor of crack ripped through his nostrils. "Damn man, y'all smoking that stank ass shit in here", Gusto exclaimed as he twisted his face up trying to relieve himself of the smell. Itty Bitty, Hook Dog, and Talk Slick sat on separate couches in the living room high as a kite. They just finished having a crack party. "Oh shit, there go my boy", Itty Bitty stated before he stood up and began doing a funny dance. Gusto's life wasn't the only one that changed for the better. Talk Slick's crack house was the most decked out spot on the block. The walls were repainted all white and brand new modern furniture decorated the living room and the kitchen. Not just that, Talk Slick, Itty Bitty, and Hook Dog were no longer bummy looking. They kept wads of cash in their pockets and dressed better than the average drug dealer. Hook Dog and Talk Slick began laughing at their friend. "Itty you shot the hell out", Gusto stated. He dug his hand into his pocket, pulled out three hundred dollar bills, and handed the money to Talk Slick. "Thanks man", Talk Slick stated. "Where my money at", Itty Bitty questioned while still dancing. Without saying a word, Gusto turned around and rushed out of the house.

Gusto parked a few houses from Shaky's crib. He smelled the mouth watering aroma of the food cooking on the grill. He also heard the sounds of the loud music coming from inside Shaky's house. Shaky was standing close near her porch with her back turned, cooking on the smokey grill. Geronimo, Lil Petie, Chopo, and a few more new found crew members were hanging around smoking weed and drinking liquor. Several months back, Shaky's house became Gusto's hot spot, so get togethers such as this was nothing unusual. Gusto, who rarely had to touch the product after buying it from the plug, lived every single day like it was a celebration. Geronimo, on the other hand, was so busy selling dope to all of the dope boys in the city. They had a thirty pack or better policy, so it was nothing but official dope boys that came to spend their money. "She must have that door wide open. That music loud as hell",

Gusto said to himself. "What you cooking on that grill girl", Gusto asked as he approached Shaky from behind, trying to look over her shoulder. She quickly turned to see that it was Gusto standing over her. She was in the middle of flipping over the ribs. "Boy don't be walking up on me like that. Like you know me or something", she stated in a playful tone. Gusto began laughing. Chameleon and three other females from around the way were seated in white plastic chairs with bottles of beer in their hand, bobbing their heads to the music. "What's up babes. You like my new ink?" He poked his chest out for a few seconds so that she could get a good look at it, and then turned around so she could see the one on his back. Chameleon stood up and learned forward. "Turn back around, let me see." When Gusto turned back around to face her, she began examining the art work that stood before her. The sight of the freshly greased up tattoos on Gusto's husky frame made her panty's moist. "Ummm, damn", she thought. "Hell yeah I like it. Whoever did it did a real good job", she said while licking her lips and looking at him with lustful eyes. Gusto noticed the way she was looking at him. "You shot the hell out", he stated. "Let me sit my black ass down before the faucet start running down my legs", Chameleon said with no shame.

By this time everyone else around started noticing Gusto's tattoo's. "Man this nigga crept off to the tat shop without us", a guy name Neef stated while standing in front of his all white Lexus. Neef, a new member of Gusto's drug team, was chubby and brown skin with gold teeth in his mouth. "Gusto you on some bullshit, you know we was supposed to go together", Geronimo stated. Everyone else began making their side comments, agreeing with Geronimo. Hearing all the side talk, Geronimo motioned his hands for everyone to calm down. "Don't even trip. We going tomorrow." "Come on man, I didn't know y'all niggas was going to take shit so serious.", Gusto stated. He handed the bag to Geronimo. "Damn, you went and got the big bottle huh", Geronimo stated. "What's good with you big bro", Chopo greeted. He wore a white tank top and a long gold chain around his neck with a huge Jesus piece medallion. "What up!", Gusto replied slapping hands with him. "We almost finished that work." "Damn y'all knocked that shit off fast as hell", Gusto was impressed. Thanks to Gusto's new cocaine connect, crackheads out North Trenton were coming to spend their money faithfully with his young hustlers. After realizing the cocaine he was getting from Lango was 100% pure, he started stretching one key in to two, and it was still extremely potent. He then gave it to his workers, ordering them to stuff crack into the baggys until they looked like they were going to bust open. The baggys went for ten dollars a piece. There was so much crack inside of them that some of the fiends smoked half the bag and sold the other half for ten, getting their money back to buy some more. "I wouldn't be surprised if y'all was making more money than me down there", Gusto stated charismatically. "Nah big bro, I don't think all of us put together getting more paper than you", Chopo stated before taking a huge gulp from the liquor bottle he was holding.

Gusto shifted his eyes to Lil Petey, and noticed that he was the only one not having a good time. "What's up Lil Petey, you alright?", Gusto asked. Lil Petey looked him dead in the eyes without showing any type of expression. "Yeah, I'm good", he lied. Gusto could tell Lil Petey was lying and that something was really bothering him. "You sure man?" "Yeah, I'm alright", Lil Petey shot back. The truth was, Lil Petey couldn't stand that he was amongst a whole bunch of dudes he considered to be soft and fake. It made him sick to his stomach. He knew all these new dudes were just pretending to be family and really didn't have Gusto's best interest in mind. They were just tagging along because he was the captain of the winning team. The only reason he came to the cookout was because Chopo kept asking him. He decided he would come, but would not stay

81

long. Gusto wanted to ask Chopo what was up with his best friend, but he decided not to push the issue.

Geronimo sat the gigantic bottle of Remy Martin on the hood of Neef's car, and made his way towards the house to get some cups for everyone. "Damn I hope it's enough cups in there", he thought. Shaky saw him coming up the steps and put her hands up, stopping him in his tracks. "Go grab the paper plates from off the top of the refrigerator for me so I can make y'all food." "Alright", he said. "Gusto, you want me to make you a plate?", Shaky asked loud enough to be heard over the music. Gusto, who was standing in the mist of everyone, nodded his head yes. He knew he was going to need to put something on his stomach before he started drinking. Geronimo finally walked back through the front door holding the paper plates in one hand, and a small bag of red plastic cups in the other. The party was jumping, and everyone had a few drinks by now. As Geronimo walked to hand the plates over to Shaky, one of the young ladies sitting on the porch reached out and grabbed Geronimo's manhood. "Wow, you wilding. Don't you see my girl down there cooking on the grill", Geronimo stated, causing the young lady to feel embarrassed and awkward. She looked over at Shaky who was already looking up at her with a huge silver fork in her hand. "Oh that's my bad Shaky. I didn't know y'all was messing with each other", she explained sounding a bit nervous. Chameleon, who was sitting on the porch as well, through her head back and burst in to a loud laughter. "Something is really wrong with that boy." Shaky remained silent, and just shook her head. She closed her eyes for a few seconds, and took in a deep breath. "This nigga just don't give up", she thought while looking at Geronimo walking down the steps. Geronimo had a sexy smirk on his face as he approached her to hand her the plates. "No matter what, I ain't never cheating. I'm content with just you", he stated in a charming way, staring deep into her eyes while licking his lips. Shaky tried her best to fight back her smile. She didn't want to admit it, but in a crazy kind of way, she liked the way Geronimo showed his affection towards her. She never had a man show her this much attention as consistently as he did. "Geronimo you know you need to stop", she stated. "Nah, you know you need to stop playing and give a nigga a shot at the title. Damn, you know I'm feeling you. What I have to do, drop down to my knees and propose to you in front of everybody." Seeing him loose his patience like that made Shaky want to see what would happen if she continued to press his buttons. "Well I guess I'll talk to you later. I about to fix these plates", she stated rolling her eyes and turning back around to tend to the food. A frustrated Geronimo made his way towards Gusto and the homies. "So what's up bro, where we at tonight", Neef asked. "You let me know and we there", Gusto replied. One of the other homies standing near by stepped up. "We at Club Maxine's tonight. Those Dip Set niggas from Harlem gonna be down there, so you know the hoes will be there too." "Well fuck it then, that's where we at tonight", Gusto stated as the crew started to get amped up.

Once Shaky handed all the females their plates, she quickly fixed a few more plates of food and went to where the crowd of thugs were standing. "Here y'all go", she stated as she approached Gusto and Neef. One of the homies looked at her with his face turned up. "Damn, where my plate at?" "It's right over there on the table, shit I only got two hands", she stated with an attitude. "Matter fact, who else want they plates go grab them off the table because I'm about to sit down and eat my goddamn food." All the females were high as hell and had the munchies from the weed they been smoking. They were trying not to scarf down their food just in case the guys were paying attention. Chameleon stopped eating and looked at Shaky. "Girl you know you need to stop playing with Geronimo and give him some play." Shaky looked at her best friend, "Now you already know that boy ain't no where near my type." "Yeah alright. I don't know who you think you fooling, but I know you. I see how you be blushing when he be all over you talking that talk." Chameleon noticed a smirk appear on Shaky's face. "Umm hum, just what I thought", she stated with her lips turned up. Shaky started laughing, "Girl you crazy." "No girl, you the crazy one. You better get him for somebody else do", Chameleon warned. Shaky stopped laughing. "You really think I should give him a shot?" "Hell yeah! I don't know what it is, but he really feeling you. I would have been given up on your ass, fuck that!" Shaky and the other females on the porch began chuckling. "Plus ain't nothing wrong with Geronimo. He got real money now, he look good as hell, and he'll make sure you don't want for nothing", Chameleon explained. "He don't seem like he ready for me though. He be acting all immature", Shaky stated as she began to watch Geronimo interact with his homeboys. "Girl once you slam that pussy on him, you're going to be able to turn that nigga into whatever you want." Shaky listened to her friend, never taking her eyes off Geronimo. Even though what she said about Geronimo was true, Chameleon was trying to hook the two up for her own personal reasons.

Later on that night, Gusto and his drug dealing crew went to the club and had a ball. They popped bottles of champagne, bought out the bar, and took pictures with the rap group that performed. Everything was going well until someone started shooting, causing everyone to stampede out of the club. One person died, and three young men were seriously injured.

CHAPTER 16: MOMMA'S BABY

Gusto pulled in front of Tayla's house and parked his Aston Martin. She had called earlier to let him know she had something very important to tell him. Gusto expected her to be outside already. "Come on man, where the fuck she at", he grumbled impatiently before beeping the horn twice. BEEP! BEEP! Ever since Gusto's money pile grew higher the relationship between him and Tayla took a turn for the worse. Because of his hood rich status, a female of her caliber became average to him, therefore he no longer appreciated her like he used to. He was very slick with his mouth now and he didn't spend as much time with her. In fact, the only times he would come through was to get some pussy, or to pick up the drugs he had her stash at her mom's house.

Tayla came walking out the front door and down the porch steps. Once she made it to the car, she got in the passenger seat. "So what's up? What do you have to tell me that's so important?", Gusto asked getting straight to the point. Tayla's heart began beating rapidly as she wondered how Gusto was going to respond to what she was about to tell him. "He might be happy, or he might be on some other shit. Oh well, it's only one way to find out", she said to herself trying to boost herself up. She looked Gusto in his eyes and told him. "I'm pregnant", she stated in an innocent tone. Gusto's eyes got big. "You pregnant? So who is it by, cause you and me ain't fuck around in months." Tayla couldn't believe what she was hearing. "What you mean who is it by? Muhfucka it's by you!" Her eyes started tearing up. "You the only person I been with for the past year, and we just had sex a month ago." "Man if you don't go head with all that", Gusto stated harshly raising his voice. "I fucking hate you!", she screamed. She was so upset her body began to shake as she cried hysterically, burying her face in her hands. She was ruined and wished she had listened to her mother when she told her: not to ever mess around with dudes that run the streets. Gusto sighed out loud. "Is that all you had to say cause I got something important to do." Tayla lifted her head up and looked at Gusto, who was sitting there with a blank stare showing no emotion. "Fuck you!" She quickly got out of the car, leaving the door open. As soon as Tayla rushed through the front door she fell right into her mother, who was watching from the living room window the whole time. "He said the baby ain't his. Then kicked me out of his car", she continued to cry hysterically.

All her mother could do was hold her daughter and try to comfort her. She then looked at her son sitting on the couch. Seeing his sister cry over some lame ass chump that wasn't man enough to handle his responsibility caused him to rage inside. "That bitch ass nigga ain't going to play my little sister out. Fuck that!" Kevin quickly rose from the couch and stormed out the front door. As soon as he stepped foot outside, he saw Gusto with his back turned closing the passenger door. Kevin leaped down the steps and rushed him full speed. Gusto heard the footsteps coming from behind, but it was too late. A wild overhand punch violently crashed against the side of his jaw that sent him staggering to the side. "Ugghh!", he grunted in pain. Slightly dizzy, he tried to regain his balance. The right side of his jaw began to swell. Kevin growled as he rushed him with all his strength and speed, forcefully tackling him to the concrete. "Muhfucka you trying to play my little sis out", he growled like a mad man with crazed eyes. He began pounding Gusto's face in like a wild gorilla, busting his nose and lip open. After the first few blows, Gusto managed to throw his arms up to guard his face. Several cars began stopping in the street to watch the fight, causing a long line of traffic. Some of the people that lived on the block heard the commotion and came outside to watch. Kevin was still trying to punch through Gusto's guard, but his hands began hurting. "Fight back you bitch ass nigga!", he stated before wrapping his huge hands around Gusto's neck and chocking him. Gusto grabbed hold to Kevin's wrist and began trying to restrain his grasp. "This nigga trying to kill me", he thought to himself as he began to feel light headed. Tayla's mother rushed out the front door. Her mouth fell open when she saw her son's heavy frame laying over top of Gusto strangling the life out of him. "Kevin! Let him go!", she screamed. She ran towards her son. "Kevin let him go!" She was frantic, she ran up behind trying to pull Kevin off with all her might. "Stop before you kill him!" Hearing his mother's screams and feeling her hands pulling on him, Kevin snapped out of the zone he was in and reluctantly released his tight grasp. Gusto desperately gasped for air in an attempt to catch his breath. He began holding and massaging his neck until he was able to roll over and get up on his knees. His head was aching, his eyes were watery, and his neck felt stiff as if he was just in a car accident. "Get the hell up and get from in front of my house", Kevin barked. He wanted to finish having his way with Gusto, but he had too much respect for his mother to continue. Gusto eventually caught his breath, and slowly stood up to his feet. His first instinct was to go to his car, grab his pistol, and let Kevin have everything in the clip. But when he noticed the traffic jam and block full of onlookers, he knew it would be an extremely stupid idea. Gusto felt humiliated knowing that everyone saw him get ragged to the floor like a helpless kitten that was snatched up by the jaws of a vicious pit bull. "You got that", Gusto stated looking at Kevin with evil eyes. His face was lumped up and his mouth was bleeding. Never taking his eyes off his enemy, Gusto got back into his car. "My sister don't need you. I'll help her take care of the baby", Kevin shouted angrily before Gusto sped off recklessly down the street. The next day, Gusto sent Chopo and Lil Petie to get at Kevin. They waited outside his house. Once Kevin came out, and

got in his car, Lil Petie and Chopo followed him. They
caught him at a red light and shot his car up, but didn't hit
him, not even once.

CHAPTER 17: NEENA AND GERMAINE

The time was 6:30 am, and even though the sun wasn't fully in the sky yet, it was still warm outside. Majority of the streets in the city were busy around this time. Everyday people going to and from work were out around this hour, as well as the dope boys who were starting their day. Gusto was driving in an all black Pontiac on his way to pick up one hundred and fifty thousand from his stash house to take to the connect in Patterson. Once he made it near the tall 620 building on West State Street, he made a left turn down a side street. He parked in front of a brick house and got out the car. He made sure to survey his surroundings before entering the house. Suddenly, a dark green Lincoln Navigator with dark tents turned down the street. "There go that bitch ass nigga car right there. I told you this was the street he turned down", Bugsy the Bulldog stated eagerly. "That nigga went in there to either grab some work or money", Ratchet Rob assured as he pulled over and parked a few cars behind Gusto's. Bugsy and Ratchet Rob were at the Ghetty gas station when they spotted Gusto driving down Calhoun Street, and had been following him every since. And being as though he was out and about at these hours they knew he was about to bust a major move.

Throughout the several months that passed by, Rob and Bugsy shot at Gusto whenever they saw him no matter where they were. Gusto always shot back, but neither one of them ever landed a shot. But now, they finally had him right where they wanted him. Meanwhile, Gusto was upstairs inside the bathroom getting one of the best head jobs he had ever received in his life. He stood in the middle of the bathroom with his pants and boxers down to his ankles while his side chick Nesha, was on her knees viciously slurping and slobbing his long rod. Nesha had a shiny butter pecan skin complexion with short hair.

"Awww shit Nesha..damn", he grunted in pleasure as he grabbed the sink. As soon as Gusto entered the bathroom to use it, Nesha came in behind him and aggressively pulled his pants down and began going to work. Without saying a word, she tightly grabbed hold to both of his butt cheeks and began bobbing her head back and forth. Her juicy oversized lips were wrapped around his thickness as if they were specially made for it. She slurped loudly and sucked for dear life as thick globs of spit fell from her mouth on to the marble floor. Feeling the tension build up in his balls, Gusto's mouth fell open as he looked up at the ceiling and let out a loud moan. Seeing how he was reacting, Nesha immediately knew what time it was. She removed one of her hands from his butt cheek and began gently rubbing his balls while working her skillful tongue on the head of his penis, twirling her tongue around it as fast as she could. She felt Gusto's but cheek tighten. "Ahhhhh!", he grunted in pure ecstasy with his lips curled up. His entire body stiffened as he exploded inside her mouth. Nesha hungrily swallowed every single drop of nut, deep throating it repeatedly, moving her head from side to side. She gagged while looking up into Gusto's eyes. Gusto felt himself get weak in the knees, but quickly got his balance by holding on to the sink tighter. He stepped back to pull his, now soft penis, from out her warm mouth. "Mmmm", she moaned, grinning while still on her knees. "Taste just like vanilla ice cream. Can I have some more?" Nesha was a certified head monster that had a serious fetish for sucking dick. Every time Gusto came over, that's all she wanted to do, and if he tried to deny her she would do exactly what she did today: hold him down and rape him with her tongue. "Come on now, I already told you I had to go take care of some serious business."

Gusto bent down to pull his boxers and pants up. Nesha began chuckling, thinking about how she ripped his pants off and pinned him up against the wall. "This bitch crazy", Gusto thought. He looked at his gold Rolex which read 7:00 am. "Yeah, I still got more than enough time." Then he turned to Nesha. "Why every time you suck me off you swallow instead of spitting it out?" "Because it's a form of disrespect", she responded before making her way out of the bathroom. Gusto followed her down the steps and into the living room. She grabbed the remote control from the table, and sat on the black leather couch flicking through the channels. Gusto leaned down and picked up the blue duffle bag filled with cash and said, "Alright, I'ma holla at you later." He turned around, walked to the kitchen and left out the back door. Gusto traveled through Nesha's backyard, jumped over a small fence, and began walking through someone else's backyard. Out of no where a huge rottweiler in the yard next door ran up to the gate and began barking. "Shut the fuck up", Gusto stated as he jumped back at the dog. He quickly walked through the side of the house, which led to the next street over. Jumping inside his white truck, he pulled off and headed towards the train station. Gusto didn't even know that there were goons outside waiting for him. Leaving out the back and jumping into another car was protocol for him whenever he was handling business.

     Gusto always used the same cab driver to escort him to Patterson, and as time passed the two began getting somewhat familiar with one another. Sometimes he could sense the driver had something against him because of the sarcasm and hint of hostility he showed during their conversations. Gusto figured it would be smart to keep it cool with the driver since he was well aware of the type of business he was in to. During most of the ride, the two conversed about sports, music, and other things that related to real life situations. "Come on now, you know you bugging for saying that", Gusto stated looking at the driver like he was crazy. "Jay Z ain't got shit on Nas." "You crazy as hell! Jay Z got more swagger than Nas and the whole

Queensbridge put together!", the cab driver shot back in a strong Jamaican accent. He was from Brooklyn, and was a Jay Z fan to the core. They were now driving down 17th Avenue, which wasn't that far from the spot. Gusto began chuckling at the cab driver's heavy accent, it sound funny whenever he got exited and tried to talk. "Yeah, you laughing because you know I'm right." Gusto face turned serious. "Nah nigga, I'm laughing because I can barely understand what the fuck you saying. Yeah Jay got swag I'll give him that, but Nas crushed that nigga when they was beefing." Gusto burst out laughing again, trying to get under the cabbie's skin. The driver knew Gusto was speaking the truth, so he decided not to challenge it. "Jay's camel looking ass was done after that, and you know it", Gusto continued. "Who got more money?" "Aww man, we was just debating about who was the best rapper, not who had the most money. I could care less about what they got, I'm trying to get my own paper. I just like the music." The driver finally pulled up in front of the restaurant. "I'll be back to get you in thirty minutes", he stated trying to conceal his anger. Gusto knew he pressed a nerve but paid it no mind. "Alright bro", he stated as he grabbed his duffle bag and climbed out of the car. "Fucking piss head drug dealers don't know shit", he grumbled under his breath while he watched Gusto stroll inside.

When Gusto stepped inside he went to the table in the back where he always sat. Neena the waitress was behind the counter talking to the other waitresses. He locked eyes with her and smiled, waving his hand smoothly in acknowledgement. A sexy smile appeared on her face and she waved back. Every time Gusto came to the restaurant he tried to gradually cut in to her, the two always had little small talk with one another. He would press his luck and try flirting with her, and to his surprise she would always blush, never giving any sign that she wasn't interested. This convinced Gusto that he had a chance with her. Gusto picked up the menu and started looking it over. He would always eat dinner before he went to the bathroom to make his transaction, this way he didn't look obvious. Neena began walking towards his table. "Hey Germain! How are you doing today?" She greeted him with a warm smile as she placed her small hand on his broad shoulder. "Did you figure out what you want to order yet?" Not only were they on a first name basis, but she noticed that every time he came to the restaurant he ordered something different, which indicated to her that he was an adventurous type of dude. "Yeah, I already know what I want. I just was sitting here trying to figure out what you might want to eat, just in case you decided to take a twenty minute break and have lunch with your boy", he stated charmingly, looking her in the eyes. Neena started to blush. "Germain you're too much." "I've been told that a few times." He waited for her to respond, but she didn't so he continued. "So what's up? You having lunch with me?" "Come on Germain, you know I can't just stop working to sit down and have lunch with you here. My co-workers and customers will look at me like I'm crazy", she said politely. "Well what about a different time and a different place", he insisted. Neena squinted her eyes and stared at him intensely. "Mmm, I don't know about you. You might not be ready for me", she stated seriously. She thought Gusto was cute, she liked the way he dressed and admired his raw and uncut ways and smooth swagger. But she also thought things would turn out bad if Flocko found out they were messing around. This left Neena feeling somewhat skeptical, but then again, Flocko did have a wife and kids. "Damn, she ain't feeling a nigga", Gusto thought. "Oh yeah, that's what you think? I ain't ready? Well I never been the type to clown around and play games, so all you have to do is give me a chance to show you I'm ready, and I'll prove it to you. How about that?", he stated. Neena kept the same skeptical expression on her face. She stared at him for several seconds and said,

"So what is it that you want to order?" Feeling like he just played himself, Gusto quickly looked back at the menu, placed his order and handed her the duffle bag filled with cash. Neena turned to take the order from an older couple sitting a few tables away, and then made her way to the kitchen.

Gusto sat at the table trying to figure out where he went wrong in his attempt to express his interest in Neena. "Damn man, she really wasn't feeling the kid", he thought. He never been rejected by a female before, so he didn't know how to accept Neena's withdraw. "I know one thing, if she fuck around and tell Flocko I tried to holla at her ain't no telling what might happen." His mind began to wonder as he thought about the risk and possibility of loosing his dope connect. "I fucked up." He noticed Neena strolling back to his table with his plate and a tall glass of lemonade. "Here you go",she stated. She pulled the bill from the front pocket of her apron, and placed it on the table. "Enjoy." She turned away from the table, and continued handling her work duties. Before Gusto picked up his fork, something told him to look at the bill. That's when he noticed her cell phone number and name neatly written on it. A wide grin spread across his face. "Oh she was feeling the kid", he thought feeling relieved.

Once he finished his meal, Gusto went to the bathroom and grabbed two huge duffle bags each filled with two hundred and fifty packs of dope. Once he stepped outside, he saw the yellow cab coming down the street. Gusto climbed inside and was ready to take his trip back to Trenton. Although Gusto reaped the benefit of being charged a hundred dollars a pack, and was getting hit off with consignment to match whatever he purchased, he still made the unwise decision to short Flocko ten thousand dollars on each re-up. The first time was a mistake, but since Flocko never mentioned it, Gusto intentionally did it each time after that.

94

CHAPTER 18: BILLIE JEANED

It was entirely too hot outside so instead of sitting on the porch like usual, Geronimo, Shaky, and Chameleon decided to stay inside to smoke their blunt of weed. The air conditioner hooked up in the window was on full blast, giving the entire downstairs a fresh and cool feeling. Two cream colored suede couches were neatly positioned in the living room. A 54 inch flat screen tv hooked up to a surround sound system sat in the entertainment center. There was a huge portrait of Shaky's mother who passed away a few years ago hanging on the wall. "Damn girl, what you trying to do, take the blunt to the head? Pass the weed", Chameleon stated while sucking her teeth looking at Shaky who was sitting next to Geronimo. "My bad girl. I was so caught up in this good ass movie, I ain't even know I was chiefing." Shaky took another pull of the blunt before passing it to Chameleon. They were watching Friday After Next, and this was Shaky's first time seeing it. She was tuned all the way in, loving every minute of it. "Umm hum. You sure it was just the tv?", Chameleon stated. "Yeah I'm sure, what else would it be?" "Girl please just stop it. I noticed how you be on your lovey-dovey-I'm-with-my-man-right-now mode when Geronimo come around." Shaky held back her reaction. "I ain't even going to feed into your mess. I'm just trying to enjoy the movie." Geronimo began rubbing his hand on her inner thigh. Shaky finally gave him a shot, and he was doing everything in his power to convince her that he wanted to be her man. He was spending time with her, and giving her any and everything she wanted. Regardless of what Shaky said, Chameleon knew her almost her whole life and could tell she was starting to show Geronimo a little more attention than usual. Taking notice to how Geronimo spoiled her rotten without Shaky having to ask, Chameleon knew it was just a matter of time before he fell right into her booby trap. "Um hum, I see that smirk. I should tell him how you be talking me to death about him." She switched her voice into a nagging tone. "Geronimo this…Geronimo that…All goddamn day." Geronimo couldn't help but smile while looking at Shaky. "What she talking about?" "Baby I ain't paying her no mind." "Ya'll crazy", he stated while scooting closer to her.

Geronimo felt his phone vibrating. He looked down and noticed it was a text from Gusto. It read: I'LL BE BACK IN THE CITY IN 15 MINUTES…MEET ME AT THE SPOT. Geronimo already knew Gusto went up top for the re-up and was waiting to get word that everything was everything. Knowing exactly what time it was, Geronimo looked at Shaky. "I got to go handle some business real quick. I'll be back." Geronimo stood up from the couch. "Be careful baby", Shaky stated looking up at her man, knowing exactly what he was about to go do. Once Geronimo left the house, Chameleon took a pull on the blunt and then handed to Shaky. "So damn, y'all must be getting really close with each other." "Yeah, he's not as bad as I thought he was", Shaky admitted before taking a pull. "I told you. So that must mean he's about to be your hubby then." "Nah, I ain't say all that." Shaky wasn't that high. "Well damn, did you even give him some pussy yet?" Chameleon already figured Shaky didn't fuck him yet, because she would have already told her. She just wanted to make sure. "Nope! He ain't get none of this wet wet yet", Shaky replied. "So what the hell are you waiting for? Shit, this nigga treating you like a queen from South Africa or some shit and you still ain't give him none?" Chameleon couldn't relate, she never would have waited that long. Shaky began chuckling, feeling a bit proud of herself for holding out. Chameleon kept on. "He probably fucking up his re-up money and everything trying to buy you the whole damn world." Shaky spoke up for Geronimo. "One thing he ain't doing is fucking up his re-up money. His paper longer than train smoke." "What make you so sure", Chameleon challenged. "Because just the other day, he showed me over a hundred thousand dollars in a safe", Shaky informed. "Word up!" The thought of having that much money in her possession made Chameleon's pussy tingle. "Hell yeah", Shaky assured sounding shocked herself. "I'm surprised to hear that the way he be stunting and blowing money left and right."

After finding out exactly what she wanted to know, Chameleon's mind began racing a mile a minute. Chameleon and Gusto lived together, but she could never tell how much money he was accumulating. He never touched the drugs, and every time he collected the profit money he put it up in his stash house. The only thing she got to see was the fifty thousand dollars of pocket change he left laying around the house. And for that reason, Chameleon took on the task of hooking her best friend up with Geronimo. The hook up would give Chameleon the inside scoop on things she didn't know about her man. And from the looks of things, it was working. Shaky continued on, "I'm thinking about giving him some of this good pussy tonight, but something is telling me to make him wait a little bit longer. What you think?" "I don't even know why you asked me that knowing damn well what I'm going to say." Just then, someone began knocking at the door. Chameleon quickly got up and asked in a high tone, "Who is it?" "It's Ree Ree", the female standing on the other side of the door announced. Knowing who it was, Chameleon replied, "Come in." Ree Ree opened the door and stepped inside the cool house. "Hey what's up y'all", she stated before taking a seat on the couch. Ree Ree was brown skin and heavy set, and was Chameleon's first cousin. "I ain't see you in a nice little minute. I like your hair", Chameleon complimented smiling as she rubbed across her cousin's hair. "Thank you. I been staying low, trying to break old habits and get my shit together." "How many you want?", Shaky asked, reaching down to grab her pocketbook from off the floor. "Damn Shaky, you ain't here me when I said I'm trying to break my bad habits. I ain't come her for that. I came here to let Chameleon know about that dog ass no good man of hers named Gusto."

A look of shock and wonder appeared on Chameleon's face, and an unsettled feeling struck her in the pit of her stomach. From the way Ree Ree said it, Chameleon could tell that it was something relating to another female. "What the hell this nigga done did", she thought. Ree Ree paused for a split second when she noticed the look on her cousin's face before she continued. "Listen girl, because this is the truth and nothing but the truth. I was riding down Brunswick Avenue the other day and saw Gusto fighting my ex boy toy Kevin. Kevin was fucking him up something serious too", Ree Ree paused again to look at Shaky, who was all up in her mouth. "Anyway, once the fight was over Gusto sped off in his car. So I went up to Kev to ask him what happened, and he said that your man got his little sister pregnant and was trying to play her out saying that the baby wasn't his. Mind you, I know the family so I checked in to it. I saw Tayla sitting on the couch crying her little heart out. I asked her was it true, and she said yeah and even though Gusto's dead beat ass ain't claiming it, she still going to keep it. They family don't believe in abortions." Ree Ree finished her story. There was a deafening silence in the room. Chameleon looked at Shaky before she spoke. "No this nigga ain't running around her getting these little dirty bitches knocked up and shit." Chameleon already knew he was fucking other bitches and really didn't care too much about it, she just played along. For one, she was doing the same thing, but getting someone pregnant was a totally different ball game. It meant Gusto would be obligated to dish loads of cash out to someone else, which would interfere with her money flow.

Chameleon began mumbling ill words under her breath as she pulled her cell phone out and dialed Gusto's number. The phone went straight to voicemail. "Oh now his ass got his phone off", she growled angrily before dialing it several times more. Each time it went to voicemail. She looked back at her cousin. "Where you said the bitch live at again? On Brunswick right?" "Come on now Chameleon, don't even take it there", Ree Ree stated, knowing her cousin would try to bring the drama to Tayla's front door. "Tayla's a good little college girl that made a mistake. If anything, all that negative energy and anger should go towards Gusto's rotten ass." "I ain't on no bullshit like that", Chameleon claimed. "Shit, picture me fighting over his ass with all these niggas I got waiting in line begging to taste this pussy. I just want to see if the little bitch is on my level." Ree Ree still wasn't sure if she should give her Tayla's address. Even though her and Kevin were no longer seeing each other, she was still cool with him and his family. She didn't want to be the cause of any unnecessary drama, but at the same time she didn't want her cousin to be blind to what was going on with her so-called man. Shaky was speechless, all she could do was shake her head. Chameleon sucked her teeth. "The most I might do is ask the bitch a few questions." "Alright, I'm going to take your word for it. She live at 224 Brunswick, and if you decide to talk to her, I don't want my name coming up in nothing." "Matter fact, you know what…Let me see your cell phone Shaky." Without saying a word, Shaky handed over her phone. Chameleon dialed Geronimo's number. It rung twice before he picked up. "Yo", he answered. "This Chameleon Geronimo, where Gusto at?" "Umm, he should be meeting up with me any minute now. Why, what's up?" He could sense the hostility in Chameleon's voice. He just left them, so he figured that it couldn't be too serious. "I rather tell it to him first. You said he should be on his way any minute, so I'm just going to wait on the phone until he come."

Meanwhile, the cab driver was driving up Southard Street and made a left turn on New Willow Street. The driver and Gusto had got into a heated argument because the driver called him a fake ass hustler from small country ass Trenton. The tension filled the cab quick and they rode in complete silence. Gusto couldn't wait for the ride to end so the both of them could get the hell away from each other. "It's about fucking time", Gusto said to himself as the driver pulled up to the stash house. Gusto opened the back door, grabbed his bags of dope, and began to step out the car. Before he closed the door, he looked back at the driver and said, "If I'ma fake ass hustler, you a cold blooded sucker. You just took me every where I needed to go, bought some weed off me, and ain't get paid one cent out the whole deal." He burst in to a loud sarcastic laugh when he noticed the stupid look on the driver's face. Every time Gusto took a trip to Patterson, he gave the cab driver an ounce of weed for the ride, and sold him another ounce for a low price. The tires made a loud screech as the cab sped off down the street. "Hah, he mad as hell", Gusto stated while still standing in the street.

Gusto made it into the house, Geronimo stood up from his seat holding his cell phone in his hand. "A yo, Chameleon on the phone. She said she want to talk to you and it's important." Gusto had a unpleased and surprised look on his face. "What the hell is more important then what I'm doing now?" He hated whenever someone bothered him while he was handling business. "Man grab these bags." He handed his partner the bags, and took the phone. "Chameleon." "This Gusto", she needed to make sure. "Yeah this me, I'm right around the corner from Shaky house. I'm about to walk around there right now." Without giving her a chance to speak, he hung up the phone. He looked at Geronimo, handing him back his phone. "I'm about to go around here and see what's up with her." "Alright", Geronimo replied. Gusto was cool leaving

Geronimo at the spot, as far as he was concerned his job was done. All he had to do now was sit back and wait for his team to turn in the paper.

Chameleon sat on the couch with her arms folded across her chest, waiting impatiently for Gusto to come walking through the front door. Her cousin Ree Ree already went on her way, and Shaky, who didn't want to be around the drama, was upstairs with her bedroom door closed listening to music. The sounds of Aaliyah's song "If Your Girl Only Knew" echoed from upstairs, adding fuel to Chameleon's fire. All she could think about was the lies Gusto would say once she let him know she was aware of the little secret inside of Tayla's belly. Chameleon heard the front door knob twisting. When Gusto opened the door, he saw the angry look on Chameleon's face and immediately knew something bad must have happened. Chameleon stood to her feet. "Muhfucka don't be hanging up in my ear", she snapped as she approached him. Before he could respond, she continued. "And who the fuck is this little bitch Tayla I'm hearing you got pregnant?" Gusto was in shock, wondering how she found out. Chameleon recognized the look on his face. "Oh ya ass thought I wasn't going to find out about that didn't you." Gusto caught his composure, and started looking at her like she was crazy. "I ain't got nobody name Tayla knocked up! What the hell is you talking about?" "Oh now you trying to act like you don't know who she is after you was fighting her brother in front of their house on Brunswick!", she shouted. "Damn man, I knew somebody she knew was going to see me out there", he thought. He still stuck to the script. "I ain't say I didn't know her, I said I didn't get her pregnant." Chameleon was breathing heavy, holding her hands on her hip. Gusto wasn't sure if he should keep talking or not. Chameleon waited patiently. "Why you stop, I'm still listening", she said staring deep into his eyes, waiting to hear what lie he was going to say next. Gusto swallowed hard, glanced away, and said, "I use to fuck with the bitch a while back, but I always wore a hat when we got busy." SMACK! Chameleon smacked the shit out of him, causing the side of his face to sting. It was one thing to think that he was fucking around, but to actually hear him admit it was entirely too much for her. "What the fuck is wrong with you!", he said. Gusto could tell that she was going to swing again, so he quickly grabbed both of her arms. "Calm down!", he demanded. The two tussled with each other for a few seconds before Chameleon screamed, "Get the fuck off me." She snatched away with all her might and broke loose from his grasp. Chameleon's eyes became very watery. "You out here fucking these little dirty bitches raw getting them pregnant and shit!" The tears began rolling down her chocolate face. "Ya nasty ass better not had brought me back any diseases!" "I told you she not pregnant by me. I was wearing condoms", he emphasized every word. He knew he was caught out there, and there wasn't too much he could say. He had no choice but to let her blackout on him. "You a fucking liar", she screamed with her tears blurring up her vision. "No I'm not." "Oh yeah? So if I go ask her to come to the clinic with us after after the baby is born so you could take a blood test, it's going to come back that it's not yours?" "You damn right it's gonna come back not mine", Gusto continued to lie trying to sound convincing as possible. They went back and forth with each other for a good ten minutes before Gusto gave up and stormed out the house.

CHAPTER 19: CRACKING THE SAFE

Later on that night, two look-outs stood on each end of the long alley way while Hook Dog, Itty Bitty, Chopo, Lil Petey, and a few fiends occupied the center. They were doing what they did best, handling business. "Ya smoke crack don't ya?!", Itty Bitty mocked, smiling showing his bright yellow teeth. He was referring to two skinny female crack addicts standing in front of him. One of the females handed Hook Dog a wrinkled twenty dollar bill, and then put her hand out waiting to get served. Hook Dog reached in to his plastic bag full of stones, and served the woman her money's worth. "Ya smoke crack don't ya!" Itty Bitty was high out of his mind. Chopo and Lil Petey were standing behind a small gate in a backyard filled with junk. The two females looked at Itty Bitty before he continued. "Come on now y'all. That ain't gonna do nothing but get y'all mad." He pulled out his baggie filled with crack, and took a rock that was a little over a gram and placed it in the palm of one of their hands. "There you go right there. That's more like it", he said. The woman was overjoyed by Itty Bitty's generosity. "Awe Itty Bitty thank you so much." "You really thankful?", he stated while smirking and cutting his eye at Hook Dog. "Yes we are", the other woman added. "Well how about this, we go get a nice clean room at the motel and y'all can show me how thankful you really are." He did the double eyebrow lift. Both females began laughing. "Itty you so crazy", they both said in unison, before going on their way. Itty Bitty had a reputation for throwing big crack parties at cheap motels, and having nasty orgies. "I ain't crazy, I'm serious!", he shouted as they continued to walk away. "Y'all must've forgot about this big AK-47 in my pants. That's why y'all got up out of here like that!" "Calm down Itty man. Let's focus on getting this money", Hook Dog was annoyed with his silly ass. He always goof balled around whenever females were present. Itty looked at Hook

Dog with his face twisted up. "What you mean let's get money? Nigga I got money!", he replied in a hostile tone. "What's up with you now? We been together every single day for the last year and I ain't seen you with a female not once." Chopo and Lil Petie chuckled. "Nah, this shit ain't funny. I'm dead ass serious. I throw crack parties with all kinds of different orgies, and you always be the only one that leave. Man what's up with that?" "What do you mean what's up with that. I'm focused on getting money, fuck those bitches", Hook Dog shot back. He then noticed an elderly man approaching him. "It ain't that much being focused in the world. When was the last time you had some pussy? Or should I say the first time?", Itty began smirking. "What you trying to say, Hook Dog a virgin?", Chopo was trying to instigate. "I get more pussy than his trick ass ever even thought about", Hook Dog replied as he served the older man twenty dollars worth of coke. "I'm just about money that's all." Itty Bitty tilted his head to the side and frowned. "What you trying to say? I get money too! A whole goddamn lot of it. And I got enough crack to smoke the rest of my life. How bout that!" Hook Dog looked at his parter in disbelief. "Your black ass is so high right now you forgot I be with you everyday." The two continued going back and forth with one another making a bunch of noise, barely paying attention to their surroundings. Chopo and Lil Petey laughed uncontrollably.

Out of no where, Gusto's mother Alley Cat walked up on them without even being noticed. "If I was the police all y'all would've been locked the fuck up!", she announced standing before all of them with her hands on her hip. "Now shut up and let me get something to smoke so I can go on my way!" Immediately, everyone stopped what they were doing to look at her. They were shocked that she was able to creep up on them. Alley Cat sucked her teeth. "What y'all gonna do just stand there and look at me?" Since she was Gusto's mother, she never really had to pay for crack when she came to see them. If only they knew that her son would have told them to charge her ass just like they did everyone else.

A hug smile appeared on Itty Bitty's face when he realized who she was. "Look who we got here Hook Dog. The one and only Alley Cat." Itty pulled the crack from out of his pocket and stepped towards her to proudly grant her wish. Hook Dog shook his head and and stated, "Trick ass nigga." Out of everyone else, Itty Bitty didn't mind hitting Alley Cat off with her medicine when she requested it. The wild and super freaky nasty things she did to him whenever they hooked up had his nose wide open. "That's enough right there for you baby girl?" "Yeah, this enough from you", she replied as she looked at Chopo and Lil Petey. "Y'all got something for me?" The both of them shook their heads no. "Nah, we out here empty handed. We just making sure everything running smoothly", Chopo told her. "Well shit, y'all doing a poor job at it", she told him before turning to Hook Dog. "What about you?" She dug her finger up her nose and then wiped the snot and boogers on her dingy white shirt. Hook Dog really wanted to say no, but couldn't bring himself to do it. "Yeah, I guess I got a little something for you." Alley Cat could tell he was hesitant, but she didn't care. Hook Dog hit her off with a few more pieces. "Y'all know where my son at. I need to talk to him about something real important." Before anyone could answer, she did a loud hog spit on the ground. "Today Friday right? I think he went down to the club", Chopo informed. Gusto always went to the club on Fridays. "Perfect, now let me hurry up and go in there and grab what I came for and bounce", she thought. "Alright, see y'all later." Alley Cat smiled revealing her messed up teeth, waving her left hand while holding her fix in the other. "Damn Cat, how you gonna just rush out of here without letting me know what's up for the night", Itty was still trying to get some ass. "If this little black stank dick muhfucka don't leave me alone so I could go handle my business", she grumbled. But just to make sure she didn't burn her bridge, she quickly spun around and said with a fake smile on her face, "I'll be back through here around 4 o'clock."

Alley Cat walked up Sweets Avenue, close to where her son's house was. She observed her surroundings thoroughly, making sure no one was outside to witness the scandalous act she was about to commit. The thought of someone seeing her caused her heart to beat rapidly, but it didn't stop her. The coast was clear. Alley Cat cut through the side of his house, brushing pass several green plastic trash cans. "Alright, let's get it", she whispered to herself in an effort to shake off the nervous feeling that was slowly trying to stifle her plan. Gusto was at the club while Chameleon was still at Shaky's house, so it was perfect timing. Alley Cat grabbed the only garbage can she could find, turned it up side down making sure to sit it directly underneath the living room window, carefully stood on top of it, and opened the glass window. She quickly climbed through the window, slightly scraping her stomach and thigh on a piece of metal. Alley Cat finally landed on the carpet in the pitch black living room. She started to strain her eyes in an attempt to see in the dark, but it didn't work. "Damn it's dark as hell in here", she thought. She still didn't want to turn the light on just in case someone walked in while she was still inside. Instead she pulled out a blue lighter from her front pants pocket.

Gusto didn't allow his mother in his house too often, especially upstairs. However, a few days ago he slipped up and let her use the upstairs bathroom. This is when Alley Cat noticed a small safe in the wooden cabinet under the sink. At first she was only trying to grab a roll of toilet paper, but instead she found herself picking up the safe, shaking it around trying to see if anything was inside. She wanted to snatch it then but couldn't do it without being

106

noticed, so she told herself she would come back for it when no one was home. And that time was right now. FLICK! As soon as Alley Cat struck the lighter, a glowing flame appeared in the darkness, allowing her to see a little better. She immediately looked to the stairwell. "I hope the safe still there" she said to herself. The flame from the lighter led the way as she made her way up the stairs. Once she reached the top step, Alley Cat could tell that Gusto's and Chameleon's bedroom door was open. All of the lights were out, but the opened door still made her anxious and nervous. She decided to stick with her plan, and hurriedly went to the bathroom. Once inside, she turned the light on and went straight for the wooden cabinet. "It's still here", she felt like she hit the jackpot and grabbed the safe with both hands. As she turned to stand up, she gasped and jumped back at the sight of Gusto standing in the doorway shirtless with black pajama pants on. "How the fuck did you get in here", he barked. He couldn't believe he caught his mother red-handed trying to steal his stash. He was just about to fall asleep when he heard the sound of footsteps in the hallway. At first he thought it was Chameleon coming in the house, but when he saw how late it was he decided to get out of bed to see what was going on.

Gusto's adrenaline began to rush. He was already angry that Chameleon found out about the incident with Tayla and Kevin, so when he saw his mother trying to steal something from him he immediately went into a rage. The rage was so intense he growled like a wild dog and rushed towards her, close-lining her with all his might. "Aghh!", Alley Cat groaned in agony as his huge forearm violently crashed against her collar bone sending her flying backwards. With that one swift motion she dropped the safe and fell, cracking the back of her head on the sharp hard corner of the sink. Alley Cat's unconscious body dropped to the floor, and she laid there sprawled in between the sink and the bathtub. Gusto was still seeing red and stood over his mother's frail body. "Get the fuck..." Before he could finish his sentence, he realized his mother was knocked out cold and started to panic. "Oh shit, man she probably dead." He was hoping he didn't just kill his own mother in his house. At first, he stood there for a while unsure of what to do. After a while Alley Cat's leg began to twitch. "She still alive", he said to himself feeling relieved. He darted out the bathroom and in to his bedroom. Gusto grabbed his cell phone off the charger and dialed Lil Petey number. "Yo." "Yo, this Gusto. Hurry up and come to my crib. It's an emergency." "I'm on my way", Lil Petey replied. He could tell something serious happened. After hanging up, Gusto went downstairs to unlock the door. When Lil Petey and Chopo arrived, Gusto explained what happened and had them drop his mother off at the emergency room.

CHAPTER 20: BRUNSWICK AVE

Shaky tried to the best of her ability to talk Chameleon out of going to Tayla's house to confront her about the pregnancy. She was able to keep her away for a few days, but once the reality of the situation sunk back in, Chameleon began having second thoughts. That's when Chameleon reversed everything, talking Shaky into coming along with her. She told Shaky all she wanted to do was to ask a few questions, and to see if she was on her level as far as looks were concerned. Chameleon and Shaky sat inside a black BMW that was parked across the street from Tayla's house on Brunswick Avenue. "Come on now girl, we been out here for damn near three long ass hours waiting for this girl to come out of her house", Shaky complained. "She probably ain't even there." Chameleon sucked her teeth as she looked at her friend. "Now you know it ain't been no damn three hours." "Yes it has. We parked out here at one and now its after four", Shaky shot back in a frustrated tone. Chameleon was lost for words, but then said, "Alright damn. If she don't come within the next thirty minutes we'll leave. Now roll up." Shaky looked at her like she lost her mind, and was really tempted to check her on how she just ordered her like she was her special servant, but she caught herself remembering her best friend was going through a very serious and heart aching time.

Shaky grabbed the blunt wrap, pulled a small bag of haze from her pocket and began going to work. Cars continued to drive pass. Chameleon kept her eyes on Tayla's house, and that's when she noticed a pretty young lady open the front door. "There go that bitch there." Chameleon damn near broke her neck trying to get out the car. She almost got hit by a car trying to reach Tayla. As Chameleon got closer, she realized that Tayla was strikingly beautiful and was damn sure on her level, maybe a notch or two above it which added more salt to injury. Tayla had just

109

stepped off her porch and began walking through the front yard when she noticed the unfamiliar female approach her. "A yo, ya name Tayla", Chameleon asked. A curious look appeared on Tayla's face. "Yeah that's me, why what's up?" The two were standing a few feet away from each other. Chameleon glanced down at her stomach to see if Tayla was showing any signs of being pregnant, but she couldn't tell. "Nah cause I heard you was pregnant by Gusto and just wanted to know if it was true or not. That's all", Chameleon explained trying not to show the rage that was building up inside her. Tayla frowned at the sound of his name. "Yeah I'm pregnant by that scumbag, but he saying it ain't his knowing damn well it is." She became so angry, that she began venting without taking the time to find out who the unfamiliar girl was. She didn't even bother to ask why she was questioning her about her deadbeat baby daddy. "I don't even care because I'm going to have my baby no matter what happens. My family is going to help me take care of it." "Oh yeah, you gonna keep it", Chameleon said feeling surprised and angry at the same time. "Hell yeah I'm..." Chameleon swung a wild overhand that smashed against Tayla's forehead. Tayla let out a loud scream as the sharp pain shot through her head and stumbled backwards. Chameleon snatched her up by the hair and yanked Tayla back towards her. "Bitch you gonna get rid of this baby." Tayla was trying her best to break loose from Chameleon's grasp, but as soon as she heard what Chameleon said, she quickly used her arms to guard her stomach. "This bitch trying to kill my baby", she thought as the tears began pouring down her face. Chameleon tried to knee her in the stomach, but Tayla managed to block the blows. "Bitch move ya hands and get up." Chameleon punched her in the jaw, causing it to swell up. She then began yanking her by the hair back and forth, hoping that Tayla would stop blocking her precious unborn baby. "I got something for this bitch." The idea came to her mind to fling Tayla around so she could slam her to the ground.

Suddenly the front door to the house swung open, and Kevin stepped outside. He heard the loud commotion from the living room, and decided to see what was going on. His heart began racing when he saw Chameleon pouncing on his pregnant sister. That's when he ran up on Chameleon and swung as hard as he could. CRACK! The vicious blow crashed against Chameleon's jaw knocking her out. He turned to see his sister balled up on the ground crying with her face bruised. Kevin turned into a mad man and started stomping Chameleon out while she was still knocked unconscious. "Bitch!", he growled as tears slid down his face. "Get the fuck off her", Shaky yelled running up on Kevin with a can of mace aimed at his face. She sprayed him directly in the eyes, causing him to hold his face. Shaky leaned down to wake her best friend up. Once Chameleon gained consciousness, Shaky helped to guide her to the car. They climbed inside as quickly as the could and sped off.

CHAPTER 21: BITCHES AIN'T SHIT

Ever since the fight at Tayla's house, the beef between Chameleon and Gusto became worse. This was partly because after she told Gusto that Kevin put his hands on her, he did nothing to defend her. From that point on Chameleon considered herself as single, and was completely done with his lying dirty dick ass. Chameleon ignored all his calls and stopped coming home at night, leaving him in the bed all alone wondering what she was doing. The few times they bumped in to each other at Shaky's house Chameleon would act like she didn't even know him, leaving the house immediately as if she was allergic to his presence. Whenever she disappeared like this she was either with Fonz, who she became head over heels for, or Bizzy doing whatever came to mind openly and freely. In fact, Chameleon would purposely make sure they were seen all over town riding around drinking and smoking, kissing and touching, holding hands, knowing it would get back to Gusto in no time. Young Bizzy, on the other hand, was loving every single minute, especially after finding out from his first cousin Nay Nay that Geronimo used to boast about how he and Gusto robbed and killed Da'white for two keys of coke. Nay Nay and Geronimo used to mess around so he must have felt comfortable with telling her about the robbery. However, this was something Bizzy chose to keep to himself, never expressing to Chameleon how he really felt. He had plans on getting even, he was just waiting for the right time.

Young Bizzy pulled his silver Benz inside the 7 eleven parking lot, parking directly in front of the mini market's entrance. Chameleon sat quietly in the passenger side bobbing her head to the Jay Z song playing in the car. They had just finished having sex, so the car windows were very foggy and the two of them were covered in sweat. "Do you want me to grab you something from out of here?",

112

Chameleon asked. "Grab me a turkey sub, some chips, and a 7 up." "Okay", Chameleon stated as she got out the car to walk in the store. Young Bizzy's cell phone started to ring. He noticed it was his baby mom. "Hello." "Where the hell are you at? You was supposed to be here an hour ago!" "Give me ten minutes babe. I had to handle some unexpected business, my bad", Bizzy stated in a calm tone. "Did you get my turkey sub?", she asked. "Of course I got it. What my son doing?" Bizzy was never worried about his babymom finding out about the things he did in the streets because she was a good girl that lived in the suburbs, oblivious to it all. He did worry about her little brother who hung around in the streets but really wasn't into anything. "He over here asking for you." "Tell him I'm on my way right now." Chameleon got back in the car carrying a plastic bag. Bizzy motioned for her to be quiet, and she did just that with a frown on her face, knowing exactly who he was talking to. "Alright baby, I'm on my way right now. I'll see you when I get home." He hung up the phone. "Bitch why the fuck you call her while you with me!", Chameleon yelled, slapping him in the face. A stinging sensation shot through his cheek, causing that side of his face to turn red. "Calm the fuck down. You bugging, she called me." "Pull the fuck off and take me to Shaky's house!" Without saying a word, Bizzy pulled out of the parking lot.

Geronimo was drunk and horny as hell and only had on his black and gray Calvin Klein boxers. He was laying on Shaky's new king size bed that he bought for her. Shaky was right beside him sleep under the white sheets with nothing but her bra and panties on. He already tried to slide in her while she was sleep, but got cursed out. He still had a stiff one that would not go down for nothing. "Fuck this man, I got to bust a nut", he thought in frustration as he sat up and removed the sheets from his body. Geronimo and Shaky had sex for the first time two weeks ago, and had been getting it in almost everyday which he quickly became accustomed to. Hot and horny, he turned on the large flatscreen tv so he could watch a porno and master-bate. Before he got in to it, he heard the downstairs front door slam shut. "Who the fuck is that?", he thought. He picked up his sweatpants from off the floor and slipped them on before he went downstairs. As soon as Geronimo made it to the bottom of the stairs, he noticed that the living room light was on and that's when he saw the mouth watering sight of Chameleon on her hands and knees looking under the couch with her huge ass tooted up in the air. She had on a very short skirt with no panties on, allowing him to see everything. "Damn", he stated in a low tone. He became so aroused pre-cum began to ooze from the head of his erect penis. Chameleon noticed someone else in the room. "Oh shit, you scared the shit out of me." She grabbed her keys from underneath the couch and stood up. "What you doing up this late?" She smiled as she approached him noticing the huge bulge in his sweatpants. "I couldn't sleep", he stated letting out a light yawn. "Where Shaky at?" "Man, Shaky upstairs knocked the fuck out with a hangover. We was drinking that Remy all day long." Chameleon tilted her head, and looked right in to his eyes. "Aww, and let me guess, she didn't even get a chance to give you your sleeping medicine", she made sure to speak in a soft and sexy tone. Chameleon gently grabbed hold to is waist and began licking and sucking on his chiseled chest. A low grunt escaped from his lips. The irresistible feeling of her warm tongue exploring his upper frame caused his manhood to throb intensely as it became even harder. Geronimo slid his hand underneath her mini skirt and inserted his index and middle fingers inside of her wetness. "Mmmm", she moaned as her best friend's man began pussy popping her. He removed his fingers and put them into her mouth, making her taste her own sweet juices. In her mind, Chameleon knew she had him right where she wanted him. "Go upstairs and make sure Shaky still sleep.

I'll be ready for that big dick by then." "I'll be right back." Geronimo carefully made his way up the stairs, trying not to make too much noise.

Chameleon made her way to the couch, and pulled her cell phone from out her purse. After pressing a few buttons, she sat it on the glass table in the center of the living room and then laid down on the couch. She closed her eyes to make it look like she was sleep, spreading her legs wide open. Geronimo came quietly walking down the stairs. Once he made it to the couch, he stood over top of her for a few seconds, staring in between her legs at her fat pink vagina lips. "I'm about to suck this pussy dry", he said while licking his lips. He placed his hands and knees on the cushion of the couch near her feet, lowered his head in between her legs, and began eating her pussy like a mad man. Loud slurping sounds filled the air as he sucked and licked her slit, causing her to bust a nut in his mouth instantly. The head was so good that Chameleon's legs began to shake. Suddenly, her legs popped open and she looked down at him and spazzed out. "Boy what the fuck is you doing?!" She forcefully pushed his head from in between her legs and quickly stood up from the couch. "I'm telling Gusto and Shaky!" Still on his knees with pussy juice on his face, Geronimo looked perplexed, dumbfounded, and scared all at the same time. He was looking at Chameleon while she grabbed her cell phone from off the table. She held the phone up so he could see himself on the screen playing his part in the scene that just played out. "I want fifteen hundred a week or I'm going to show Shaky and Gusto what you did to me while I was sleep!" She been plotting this scandalous act since the day she convinced Shaky to give him a chance, and she finally got the opportunity to carry it out precisely. "You a slimy bitch", Geronimo stated with clenched teeth knowing he was caught. Chameleon could see the defeat in his eyes, and chuckled wickedly. "So what's it gonna be? My payment is going to start right now, or I'm going to have to go upstairs and show my best friend the nut shit you tried to do to me while I was sleep", Chameleon stated harshly.

The two just stood there in a face off, locking eyes with each other. Chameleon broke the silence. "Fuck it, I'm waking her up right now." She walked around the glass table to avoid Geronimo in case he tried to grab her and take the phone. "Alright hold up. Damn", Geronimo pleaded. Knowing his weak ass would give in, Chameleon spun around to face him. "The money upstairs. Wait here while I go grab it real quick." "Hurry up and go get it", she demanded impatiently moving out of his way so he could pass. Geronimo felt so stupid as he made his way up the stairs. Within seconds, he came back down with a wad of cash in his hands. "Here, that's fifteen hundred." Chameleon began counting the money. When she finished, she looked at him and said, "You better be glad that's all I want from you. Now get the hell away from me." Geronimo just stared at her as she turned around and walked back to the couch. Chameleon took a seat and began looking for the remote in between the cushions on the couch.

After a successful date, Gusto and Neena realized they had a chemistry that was out of this world, and continued to see each other at least once a week. They went to restaurants, to the movies, and a few other places. They really enjoyed each other's company. Neena was feeling Gusto and his personality. He knew how to make her laugh, and he made her feel special. Gusto was feeling her too, but mainly wanted to slide inside and see how good that Spanish pussy was. And it turned out that tonight was his lucky night, after putting in all that work he was finally about to get the treat he wanted and deserved.

Neena was completely nude as she laid her voluptuous body on the king size bed. Her legs were wide open, allowing her to play with her pretty bald pussy like

116

the undercover super freak she was. "Mmm", she moaned in a low tone. She rubbed her index and middle finger across her swollen cliterous. She cuffed one of her pretty breast in her hand and began sucking on her pink erect nipples. An intense feeling of pleasure shot through her body, and she began popping herself spreading her legs even wider. Gusto, oblivious to what Neena was doing, was in the bathroom taking a shower. This little trip away from Trenton with Neena was exactly what he needed to help take his mind off all the bullshit he was going through. From him hearing all kinds of shit about Chameleon, to his mother being in a deep coma because of what he did the night he caught her breaking in to her house.

Gusto finally walked out the bathroom with a white towel wrapped around his waist. He immediately stopped in his tracks when he saw Neena on the bed touching herself. "Oh shit." Gusto's manhood grew hard instantly. "Damn, that's how you doing yours?", he stated while licking his lips with lust in his eyes. He snatched the towel off and made his way towards her. "I'm about to bust ya ass", he stated eagerly. As soon as he made it to the edge of the bed, she grabbed his manhood and began licking and sucking it sloppily. Gusto grunted in pleasure, placing his hand on her head and rubbing on her silky black hair. Neena placed her free hand in Gusto's mouth, making him taste her sweet juices. Gusto began licking her wet fingers, driving her wild. "Mmmm", she moaned as she stopped and looked up at him. "Lay down so I can sit on your face while I suck that dick", she demanded. Without wasting one second, Gusto did exactly what he was told. Neena sat her fat pussy on his face and began slobbing his knob like her life depended on it. Neena had back to back orgasms and squirted all over his face. When he busted his nut, she made sure to swallow every drop and continued sucking his dick until he couldn't take it any more. Neena laughed at Gusto's sensitivity to her tongue. Feeling like he had to redeem himself, he snatched her up and began busting her ass all over the hotel suite in every way imaginable, causing her to scream and cum all over the place. The sex was so good, the two couldn't get enough of one another. They stayed in the hotel for two days having unforgettable sex. Neena and Gusto were hooked to one another, like fiends to heroin.

CHAPTER 22: SCANDALOUS

It was just getting dark outside, and Shaky and Chameleon sat in the white plastic chairs on the porch smoking and getting high. "When he pulled down his pants and I saw what he was working with I bust out laughing right in his face", Chameleon said to Shaky. "It was soft too, so it was about half the size of my pinky." She raised her pinky up to give a better idea of what she was talking about. Shaky was laughing and enjoying her best friend's story about yet another sex-capade. "It ain't funny, I'm dead serious. While he was fucking me it felt like he was grinding up against my pussy." Shaky started laughing even louder. "You shot the hell out. You know you need to stop playing Young Bizzy out like that." "I ain't trying to play him out. I'm just keeping real. Shit, if he got a little winky dick, he got a little winky dick. I know you be wanting to bust a nut." Shaky took a pull off the weed and passed it to Chameleon. "You ain't never try to talk to him about it?" "Talk to him about what?", Chameleon was surprised that Shaky would even ask her something like that. "Nah, you know what I mean. Like try to get him to take some enhancement pills or something. I know you be wanting to bust a nut."

Chameleon wanted to let out another laugh, but smirked instead as she glanced at the burgundy Pontiac drive pass the house and up the street. "Nah girl, I ain't never say nothing to him about it. Must I remind you that I don't like taking it in the back door for nothing. But his wee wee so small, I make him stick it in my ass and then play with my pussy whenever I want to bust a mean nut." Shaky shook her head. "You a better woman than me because I would've told his ass something has to give." "That ain't about nothing because my undercover hubby got a anaconda hanging between his legs", Chameleon boasted. "Who you talking about?", Shaky asked as a puzzled look appeared on her face. "Oh you know who I'm talking about. The mighty Fonz!", Chameleon announced as if she was talking over a loud speaker. "Girl you crazy", Shaky stated. "I ain't crazy. He crazy for sticking that long double barrel shotgun in me the way he do. Shit, the last time we fucked it felt like it was about to come up my throat!" Shaky couldn't believe it. "Come on now, it can't be that damn big." Chameleon threw both her hands in the air. "I lie to you not. If it ain't that big, it damn sure feel like it." She had a flashback of how she was screaming and running the last time her and Fonz had got it in. She talked about Fonz, whom she was feeling like crazy, to Shaky but never introduced the two to each other. Fonz told Chameleon that he didn't want to meet her friends or anyone else she dealt with.

Chameleon was so head over heels for Fonz it was ridiculous. He treated her completely opposite from how Young Bizzy, Gusto, or anyone else she ever dealt with. He would talk slick to her whenever she got on his nerves, and treated her like the average hoodrat chick. And for Chameleon, his wish was her command. Fonz's nonchalant and somewhat disrespectful attitude made her like him even more. "Well shit, why I ain't never meet him then if...", Shaky stopped in mid sentence when she saw Geronimo pull up in front of the house in a black Benz truck. "Oh your little hubby popped up on you so now the cat got your tongue huh", Chameleon stated before looking at Geronimo as he got out the car and started walking to the porch. "What's good", Geronimo stated dryly while standing next to Shaky. "Hey baby." Geronimo lowered his head and gave her a kiss on the lips. "What's wrong baby? You don't seem like yourself", Shaky was concerned and could tell something was wrong. Guilt and anger always consumed Geronimo whenever he came around Shaky and Chameleon was present. "Ain't nothing wrong baby, I'm good." RING! RING! RING! The house phone began to ring. "Girl I know you hear that phone ringing", Chameleon stated. "Oh shit,

I'll be right back", Shaky said before she quickly darted inside the house. As soon as Chameleon felt Shaky was in the house far enough she looked at Geronimo with devious eyes. "Where the fuck my money pussy. You a day late, don't make me up the price." This was the first time Geronimo slipped up with the payments, but Chameleon made sure she came at his neck just to remind him that she wasn't playing any games. "Damn man, I got it right here. Chill out." "Well hurry up and give it to me before she come back out here." Geronimo's heart began beating rapidly at the thought of getting caught. He dug in his front pocket, pulled out the wad of cash, and handed it to her. Chameleon quickly leaned down to put the money in her purse. She was able to collect $65,000 from all the scandalous things she been doing to men, and planned on squeezing at least $35,000 out of Geronimo before she let him live.

Shaky finally came walking back through the front door. "Who was it?", Chameleon asked like nothing ever happened. "Oh that was my cousin Melody asking me if I want to go to the club tonight. I told her I wasn't beat." "I know that's right. Those corny ass niggas in there ain't going to do nothing but start fighting anyway", Chameleon stated. She took a pull off the blunt, and blew the smoke in the air. "I don't understand it, they see each other every single day out here in the street and don't do shit. But as soon as it's time to go out and have a good time they want to start the drama." Shaky looked at Geronimo, who was standing quietly beside her. "Damn baby, whats up? Why you just standing there looking like that?" "Nah, I was just waiting for y'all to finish talking so I can let you know that I was gonna come in a little late tonight. I'll be at the club with Gusto popping bottles", he explained. "Oh really", Shaky stated, sounding displeased. "So you just going to leave me in the house all alone huh." "I ain't leaving you alone. I'm just going to be home a little later than usual, that's all. I'll be in like one o'clock." Shaky's faced tightened. "Alright baby, twelve o'clock", Geronimo stated. Shaky just stared at him for a few seconds and sucked her teeth. "Alright, damn." Geronimo could tell she was upset, so he leaned down and kissed her on the forehead and said, "I'll see you later on."

CHAPTER 23: ONE WAY STREET

Later on that night Geronimo was at the club holding two wads of cash in the air shouting, "We get that long money over here!" A group of well dressed young ladies strolled pass him and Gusto. Gusto was sitting on a bar stool with a huge bottle of Rose in his hand, bobbing his head to the music, observing the huge crowd of people. "Come here", Geronimo demanded after he noticed one of the females smiling at him and checking out the money in his hand. The female pointed at herself with a surprised look on her face, and then said "Who me?" When she stopped, all of her friends stopped as well. Geronimo read her lips. "Yeah you, come here." The young lady made her way to Geronimo and began talking to him. Gusto shook his head at his boy, and turned around on the bar stool, facing the counter. Gust was in a bad mood. He was still hearing all kinds of rumors about Chameleon, plus he just found out that the doctors pulled the plug on his mother since she wasn't showing any signs that she would come out of the deep coma she was in. Even though Gusto despised his mother, he still felt guilty and was debating on paying for her funeral. He came to the club tonight in hopes that it would help him take his mind off of things. "This nigga crazy, he better fall the fuck back. If Shaky pop up in here and catch him talking to ol' girl he gonna be in the same predicament I'm in", Gusto thought to himself. He put the champagne bottle to his lips and took a huge gulp. The sweet taste tingled on his tongue before traveling down his throat.

Geronimo started tapping Gusto on his back, turning his head to look back at Gusto through the corner of his eye. "I see ol' girl peoples over there reckless eyeballing, you mind as well call her over here and throw her in the bag." Gusto looked up and saw a brown skin female with a stylish short haircut standing a few feet away, looking dead at him with a sexy smirk on her face. "Nah, I'm good bro. I just came down here to have a few drinks and that's it." The pretty yellow bone female bartender was coming his way with a fifth of Hennessy in her hand. "What's wrong Gusto, you alright? It look like something's bothering you." "I'm good, let me get a shot of Henny", he stated dryly as he glanced at her huge breast that looked like they were going to bust out of her tight white short sleeve shirt. She leaned down and grabbed a double shot glass, sat it on the counter, and filled it with liquor. "There you go." Gusto grabbed the shot glass and threw it back. "Ugghh", he growled as the burning sensation shot through his chest. He put the glass back on the counter. "Let me get another one." The bartender filled the glass back up with the brown liquor. "Boy you gonna fuck around and burn a hole in your chest", she stated. Gusto took the second shot down, this time it didn't burn as much. He reached into his pocket and pulled out two crisp twenties, handing them to the bartender. An older man that was sitting at the opposite end of the bar yelled, "Aye bartender, let me get six double shots and three cokes on the side." "Do you need anything else Gusto?", she asked. "Nah, I'm good for now. Thanks." She turned around to serve the other people at the bar. Gusto watched her huge booty jiggle as she marched away, before lifting the bottle of Rose up to his lips, guzzling it down like it was water.

The song switched up and the new Fat Joe song, Lean Back, starting playing causing everyone in the club to get hype. People were rushing towards the dance floor where they moved to the rhythm of the beat. Gusto remained in his same position, while Geronimo was dancing close with the young lady he was talking with. Gusto felt like he had to take a piss, so he began maneuvering his way through the crowd towards the restroom. Once he relieved himself, he started walking back to his seat. Something told him to turn to his left, and once he did he couldn't believe who he saw mixed in the crowd dancing with a female. "Check this bitch ass nigga out", he stated in a low tone. He squinted his eyes and his heart burned with rage. He quickly went back into the bathroom, pulled out his cell phone, and dialed Lil Petie's number. The phone rung several times before Lil Petie finally answered. "Hello", he answered sounding half sleep. "A yo, this Gusto. I want you and Chopo to come down to Maxine's right now, and bring those things with you. Some shit need to get handled." "Alright, we'll be there", Lil Petie assured. He hung up and exited the restroom, walking in the opposite direction from where Young Bizzy was getting his dance on.

Once he made it back to the bar area, he made eye contact with Geronimo, and motioned his hand for him to come over. Geronimo put the young lady on hold, and walked over to see what was up with his friend. "What's good?" He noticed Gusto's had a serious look on his face. "Yo, I just saw that sucker ass nigga Young Bizzy on the other side of the club. I already called Lil Petie and Chopo, so they should be on their way right now. Fuck that, he got to go." "What?!" Geronimo was puzzled. Gusto could sense that Geronimo was a little shook up. "Nigga you heard me. Young Bizzy here, so be on point cause we gonna follow that nigga home when he leave. The goons already on they way." Geronimo didn't have to ask why Gusto was so eager to get at Young Bizzy, he was well aware of the rumors too. "This nigga out here fucking everybody else's bitch, but as soon as somebody fuck his girl he wanna sick the goons on them. That's some weak ass shit", Geronimo thought to himself. Geronimo didn't want to have anything to do with what was about to go down, but wasn't man enough to speak his mind. He just went with the flow, and nodded his head in agreement. "Alright, just let me know when you ready." As soon as Geronimo turned around and began walking back to the female, Gusto stated "Don't go too far." He began analyzing the situation. "I know Young

125

Bizzy ain't in here by himself", he thought. He turned back to the area where he saw his enemy. "Where that bitch ass nigga go that fast." His eyes began scanning the huge crowd of people that occupied the club. He then spotted Bizzy, whose white and grey designer shirt stuck out like a sore thumb, buying bottles from the bar on the other side of the club. "Yeah nigga, get drunk and off point", Gusto thought as an evil grin appeared. He then started looking to see if any members from his crew were there, but he didn't see anyone.

Twenty minutes later, Lil Petey texted Gusto to let him know that him and Chopo were in the parking lot waiting in a black truck with black tents. That's when he gave the signal to Geronimo, and they both slid out making sure not to get noticed by Young Bizzy. The truck was parked on a perfect angle on the far end of the parking lot, giving them the ability to see who exited the club. After waiting a while, Geronimo began rocking his legs back and forth. "Man I got to take a piss." Gusto frowned and said "You gonna have to hold that shit." Chopo sat in the driver seat and began to shake his head. "This scary ass nigga about to piss on himself" he thought. "I can't man, it feel like I'm about to pee on myself." Gusto sighed out loud. "What time is it Chopo?" Chopo looked at the clock. "It's ten minutes 'til two." "Go head and piss man, and hurry up", Gusto ordered, knowing they had ten more minutes before they club ended. Geronimo opened the door to relieve himself outside. In the middle of him buckling his pants he heard Gusto. "There go that nigga right there. Get back in the car." Geronimo turned to jump back in the backseat. Young Bizzy was walking in the midst of several crowds of people. He eventually separated, making his way to the side of the building where he climbed inside of his black BMW. "Go head, pull off. Don't get close up on him. I know his scary ass probably be looking in his rear view every few seconds." Without saying a word, Chopo followed Bizzy through South Trenton, then through North Trenton, and was now trying to keep up with him without being noticed. By this time, they were in West Trenton and it seemed like Bizzy was just cruising though the town. "Where the fuck is this nigga going?", Lil Petey exclaimed in frustration. He was reading everyone else's mind. CLICK! CLACK! He cocked back his black 40 caliber handgun. "I'm ready to go in!" "Calm down and just be patient lil bro. He probably about to turn down one of these side streets and park", Gusto stated. Chopo noticed the red break lights on the BMW as the car made a left turn off of West State Street. "He just turned down a one way", Chopo announced. The time they been waiting for finally arrived. The BMW slowly backed into a parking spot further down the street, while Gusto and his crew slowly drove down the street and parked a few cars down from their prey. "Ya'll think he saw us?", Chopo asked. "Nah, hurry up before he get out the car", Gusto stated urgently as he reached out to open his door. RAT!TAT!TAAT!TAAAT!TAAAAT!TAAAT!TAAAT! TAAAT!TAT!. Tiny particles of glass from the window flew every where, as a storm of bullets chewed through the car. Scared for dear life, and completely caught off guard, everyone in the truck began ducking for cover as the masked man dressed in all black continued to let loose his wooden and metal AK-47 assault rifle. No one saw the gunmen when he popped up from the side of a house on the street. What they did see was the dark red flames dancing around the tip of the gun barrel. RAT!TAT!TAAT!TAAT! TAAT! He let off a few more shots until he saw that the entire truck was riddled with bullet holes. The gunman turned and ran back through the cut as fast as he could, disappearing into the darkness.

During the shootout, Young Bizzy pulled off laughing. When he realized he was being followed, he called his top goon Bugsy the Bulldog to let him know what was going on. That's when Bugsy told him where he and his infamous street sweeper would be waiting.

CHAPTER 24: BRICK BY BRICK

Chameleon and Fonz just finished having sweaty out of control sex in the backseat of Fonz's new Lincoln Navigator for two hours straight. The truck had dark tents, and they were parked on a dark side street in North Trenton so they had no worries of being caught. "Damn that dick good", Chameleon stated breathing heavily looking at Fonz. Fonz was putting his clothes back on, and remained silent. It was hot and muggy, and both of their body's were covered in sweat. Fonz chuckled. "You shot the hell out." "I ain't shot out, I'm serious. That dick priceless, all the money in the world can't add up to it. Me and you gonna be fucking until the day I die." Chameleon's coochie was aching and her right leg was still shaking. Fonz vicious pipe game caused her to have back to back orgasms that were so powerful it left her with a lingering quiver.

Chameleon used her hand to wipe the beads of sweat from her forehead. Feeling weak in the knees, she slowly climbed back in to the passenger seat to join Fonz in the front. She inhaled and exhaled, trying to relax herself as she leaned her head back on the head rest. "Now I need me some weed so I can calm my nerves. Drive to the gas station so I can grab a few wraps and something to drink", she stated while fixing her wild hair in the mirror. Fonz backed the truck up, and pulled out of his parking spot driving towards his destination. Once he made it up the hill he stopped at the corner of Race Street and the boulevard. He heard the loud sound of cop sirens, but when he looked in his rearview mirror he didn't see anything. Suddenly, they saw six patrol cars with their blue and red sirens flashing speed pass going down Southard Street. "Oh shit", Fonz stated. "Damn, I wonder where the hell they going this time in the morning", Chameleon said. If only she knew they were rushing to help Gusto and his crew. Fonz looked at the clock, it read 2:45 am. "Damn, it's that late", he said to himself. It didn't seem like they were having sex for that long. He was hoping Chameleon didn't forget the true reason why they hooked up with each other tonight. "If she don't say something about it by the time we leave from the gas station, I'm going to say something. I know one thing, her ass better not made that shit up just so a nigga could come scoop her", he thought. He knew Chameleon liked him and was well aware of her scandalous ways.

When Fonz pulled inside the Ghetty gas station, he noticed a tall husky brown skin man with a dirty white t-shirt on, standing on the side of the gas attendant window. "What the fuck is he out here waiting on?", Fonz stated as he parked beside the gas pumps. Chameleon got out the car and walked to the booth. Two Arab men were sitting inside with their backs turned away from the window watching tv. KNOCK!KNOCK! Chameleon knocked on the window, trying to get their attention. One of the men got up. "Yes, may I help you." "Yeah um, let me get two blueberry blunt wraps, an iced tea, and a pack of twizzlers." She took a ten dollar bill from her purse and slid it through the hole at the bottom of the window. While the attendant put the items in the bag, the rough looking man walked closer to Chameleon and stared at her. "What type of shit this crazy looking man on", she thought to herself. "Here you go miss", the attendant stated as he handed her her things through the slot. Once she grabbed the bag, that's when the strange man got closer. He tried to speak but his words were slurred, making it hard to understand what he was saying. "You better back the fuck up!", Chameleon barked right before she noticed the tubes connected to his ears. Fonz, who was watching from the car, hopped out the drivers seat. "Do we got a problem?" The man stood there now looking at Fonz who was walking towards him with his fists balled up. The man tried to talk again, this time motioning with his hand to show he was asking for money. "Chill baby, I think he deaf. He just asking for a couple dollars." Fonz stopped in his

130

tracks, calming down to take a another look at the situation. Chameleon gave the man her left over change. "Here you go." She turned to look at Fonz. "I told you."

They both made their way back inside the car. Fonz looked at Chameleon and said, "You lucky you saved him because I was about to beat the brakes of his ass." Chameleon began to giggle, she liked how wild Fonz was. "You crazy. Here, I got you something to drink." Fonz started drinking the iced tea, and looked at Chameleon for a while. "So what's up with that move we supposed to be making tonight?" Chameleon looked at him with a puzzled look. "What move?" Fonz's temperature began to rise, thinking she was bullshitting. "The move you called me and told me about before I came to pick you up." Chameleon was still caught up, and really forgot, she had to think for a minute. "Oh shit, my bad baby. That good dick gave me amnesia." She continued to blush while Fonz continued to stare at her impatiently. "Hurry up and go down Ingram Ave, down by Martin Luther King Park", she stated. Fonz placed one hand on the steering wheel and pulled off.

Fonz drove down Ingram Ave with Chameleon in the passenger's seat surveying the dark area. "Once you get to the bottom of the hill, make a left turn and park." Chameleon pulled out a brick from her purse. Once Fonz made the left turn, they saw a black Honda parked in front of a vacant blue house. "Alright now listen, as soon as I bust the window I'll pop the trunk. Hurry up and grab the bags out of it because I'm almost sure it's an alarm on the car", she instructed. Chameleon and Fonz climbed out the car and quickly walked across the street. Chameleon took her position near the driver side door and waited for Fonz to get to the trunk. The thought of getting caught caused her to get nervous. Her heart rate increased as she slowly cocked her hand back, holding the brick in her hand, and threw it with all her might. The brick crashed through the window, causing the car alarm to go off, echoing throughout the entire block. Chameleon reached her hand through the window to unlock the door, and then reached down to pull the lever to pop the trunk. Fonz instantly grabbed two duffle bags from the trunk and ran back to the car. "Come on", he stated urgently. Chameleon darted off by his side, and they both climbed inside the car and sped off.

CHAPTER 25: FROM BAD TO WORSE

Chopo laid on his back in a hospital bed with an all white paper night gown on. He slowly opened his eyes, to find Gusto and Geronimo standing over him. "Lil bro, what's up? You alright?", Gusto was happy to see he was finally up. The doctor just left the room and already told Gusto that Chopo's surgery went well, but Gusto wanted to make sure. He was shook up being as though Little Petey died at the scene last night. Chopo remained silent for a moment and then said, "Yeah I'm good." He tried to sit up but couldn't, as an extremely sharp pain shot up the center of his back. "Ahhh!", he yelled in agony as he fell back down on the bed. Gusto placed his hand on Chopo's chest. "Hold up lil bro. What you doing?" Chopo began squirming in the bed. "What the fuck wrong with my body!" He tried to move his left arm but it wouldn't move. "Listen, sit still and don't move like that", Gusto demanded. "I'm about to tell you what's wrong, but you have to chill." Chopo had no choice but to calm down. "You got hit up bad, the doctor said there was a 50/50 chance you wouldn't make it through surgery. They said it's going to be a few weeks for your body to heal so you're going to be stuck here until then." Gusto looked at Geronimo, who was so thankful he was not in Chopo's or Lil Petey's shoes. "Where Lil Petey at? And why I only can move one of my arms?", Chopo asked. Gusto inhaled and exhaled, trying to find a way to break it to him. "Lil Petey dead Chopo, and so is your arm. You got hit with an AK in your shoulder, hip, elbow, and your head. They had to cut through your head to get the bullet out."

Gusto knew Chopo would take his best friend's death hard. After hearing the news, Chopo closed his eyes and thought about his homie. He was so fucked up about Lil Petey dying that it really didn't register that his arm was going to paralyzed for the rest of his life. Chopo looked up at the ceiling, his vision became blurry as tears started filling up. He looked at Gusto and Geronimo, who was looking back at him. "Man if it wasn't for this nigga Gusto, none of this would have ever happened", he thought as the intense feeling of anger and sadness began to consume him. He was right, the two friends were somewhere else minding their own business when they got the call from Gusto. "Yeah, Lil Petey is dead and gone. Don't stress yourself over that though, just be glad that you're still here." Gusto tried to lift his spirit, but it was all in vain. Gusto did feel guilty about the incident, but the fact that Young Bizzy was fucking his main girl, and now had two up on him by slaughtering one of his soldiers made Gusto want to seek revenge even more. "That bitch ass nigga going to pay for this", he thought furiously. Meanwhile Chopo's blood was still boiling, he thought about speaking on it but he decided not to.

Suddenly, Gusto felt his phone vibrating. "Man this shit better be important. Who this?" "This Neef, I just seen what happened on the news. You alright?" "Yeah, I'm good. I'm at the hospital now kicking it with Chopo. He just made it through sugery." "Damn. So I know you probably ain't gonna have time to make something happen for me huh?", Neef asked hoping he could get a couple packs of heroin. He just sold his last pack, and the money was still coming in like crazy. "Come on man, you should know better than that. I always got time for that." Gusto nodded at Geronimo. "Ok cool, it's the same thing with me. I'll be parked in front of Shaky's crib", Neef stated. "Say no more." Gusto hung up with Neef. "A yo go serve Neef real quick, he parked in front of Shaky's." "How much do he want", Geronimo asked. "The same amount he usually get." Geronimo nodded his head, and left out the hospital room.

Once Geronimo exited the hospital, he got inside his car and went to the stash near MLK park. The hospital wasn't that far away, so it only took a few minutes to get there. "Damn man, I hope it ain't a lot of people out here", he thought to himself. He made the left turn on to the side street. Normally, Geronimo would have just made the quick run to one of the other stash houses but he sold it all, this was the last stash they had left. Not only that, this was a location he only liked going to at night, just to avoid being seen. As Geronimo slowly drove down the street, he made sure to pay close attention. He noticed a group of teenage kids walking towards the park. "Let me hurry up and grab this shit while nobody out here." When he got near the parked Honda, he slammed on the brakes. His eyes grew wide and his stomach dropped to the floor. Speechless, he got out the car and rushed to the trunk of the Honda. When Geronimo saw that the two duffle bags were missing, he felt like he was about to have a nervous breakdown. "Man what the fuck!" He slammed the trunk, and started looking around in a panic. "I can't believe this shit", he thought to himself as he just stood there. Things just went from bad to worse. Just last night he had almost lost his life over a chick that was getting him for major money, and now he finds that someone robbed him and Gusto for seven hundred packs of dope. Geronimo was worried and a bit nervous, not knowing what to expect from Gusto or how he would react. He knew he had to tell him, and there was no need to prolong the inevitable. Geronimo dialed Gusto's number. "What's good bro", Gusto answered. "Man somebody just robbed us for everything", Geronimo said. "What!" Gusto was hoping that he heard wrong. "Somebody jacked us for everything", Geronimo repeated himself. "What the fuck you mean! How the hell that happen?" "Man I don't know, but it happened. I'm standing here right now." "Stay right where you at. I'm on my way over there." The two hung up.

Geronimo pulled a black and mild cigar and a lighter out his pocket. He began smoking in an attempt to calm his nerves. "I wonder who the fuck did this shit", he thought. Several minutes later, Geronimo spotted Gusto down the street speed walking towards him looking like a raging bull. "That was fast. What the hell he do run down here." Without saying a word, Gusto walked up on the Honda and began surveying it. He saw that the driver side window was open, and tiny pieces of shattered glass was all over the seat and floor. "There's only two things that could've happened. You told somebody about our stash, or somebody followed you when you was making a move", Gusto accused. "I ain't tell nobody nothing", Geronimo lied with a straight face. "And nobody couldn't have followed me. Trust that, I always watch my rearview when I'm handling business." "Well how the fuck somebody know where our stash was at?" Gusto was so mad that small amounts of spit flew out his mouth every time he spoke. Geronimo stood there with a dumbfounded look on his face. "How the fuck they know where it was then! What you can't hear now?" Gusto snatched Geronimo up by the collar of his shirt. Scared to death, Geronimo quickly threw his hands up in the air. "I don't know Gusto. I don't know!" With the amount of dope that was stolen, Geronimo knew that Gusto was liable to do anything. The last thing he wanted was for Gusto to think he was the cause of their loss. Gusto's cell phone began to ring. Geronimo felt relieved as Gusto finally let his shirt go. "Hello", Gusto held the phone to his ear. "What's good big bro, it's Bubby. I'm trying to holla at you", the voice on the other end stated. "Yeah well some bullshit happened. You're gonna have to give me a day or two." "Damn man word up?", Bubby replied sounding disappointed. "Yeah man. I'll call you when everything situated", Gusto stated as he hung up, focusing back on Geronimo. "Man we got to hurry up and get some more fucking work. That was Bubby calling trying to spend some money." Gusto started hearing the sounds of voices, which made him turn and look down the street. That's where he saw a gang of kids walking in his direction. "Come on man, lets get the fuck out of here."

Gusto had to do something, and do it quick. All of his customers were calling in to request their usual orders, and the last thing he wanted was to have them spend their money else where. Without wasting any time, Gusto contacted his supplier so he could put in a special order. A special order because he just took a five hundred pack, and was in serious debt with his connect for not keeping up with his consignment payments. Gusto decided to spend his entire hand with the connect in order to quickly make back the money he just lost.

CHAPTER 26: BLITZED IN THE FOURTH QUARTER

Gusto sat silently in the back of the yellow taxi cab. He looked out the window as he rode through the busy downtown area of Patterson. On his lap sat a large black duffle bag filled with three hundred and fifty grand. "I wish he would hurry up and just get me to where I'm going", Gusto thought to himself. He started to get frustrated after he noticed the cab driver took the long way. "Can you speed it up, I'm on a time schedule today", Gusto told the driver. The driver stopped singing to the song playing in the car. "Oh shit, my fault Gusto", the driver smirked pretending to regain his focus. The driver abruptly slammed his foot on the gas, and began recklessly speeding through the traffic.

Minutes later, the driver finally pulled in front of the restaurant. Gusto climbed out without saying a word. As soon as he stepped inside, he spotted his Spanish love who was wiping down tables. She looked up to see who came in the door, and began smiling when she saw that it was Gusto. Gusto shot her a smile, and continued to make his way to his table. Despite the stressful past couple of days, the sight of Neena brightened up his mood. Neena approached the table. "Hey baby", she greeted him cheerfully. "What are you doing here on a Monday? You usually stop by only on Friday's." She sat down in the chair across from him. Every since that night when Gusto put it down, Neena was hooked like a crack addict who took their first hit and was now chasing that same high. Gusto was still feeling her, but his thirst subsided a little after she let him hit a couple of times. Gusto began to explain, "A whole bunch of bullshit happened, and I had to make an emergency move." "Damn honey, you alright? I hope it wasn't that bad." Neena began wondering why she had not been informed that Gusto was on his way. "Yeah I'm good baby. Don't worry yourself about me, I'll bounce back", he assured. Neena noticed an elderly grey haired Spanish woman several tables down waving her hand, trying to get her attention. "Baby I'll be right back. You want the same thing you always get right?" "Yeah."

Once Neena came back with Gusto's food, she sat down and chatted with him while he ate. The two made arrangements to link up during the weekend. Gusto had just finished his meal and was full as a house. He was ready to take care of his business and head back home. Gusto held up his hand to check his gold Rolex for the time. It read 4:28. "Let me hurry my ass up, the cab should be pulling up in another 2 minutes", he stated in a low tone. He stood up, wiped himself off, and grabbed his duffle bag from off the floor. Gusto entered the restroom and went to the the stall that had the BROKEN sign taped on it. Once inside, he removed the toilet, which revealed a large hole in the wall, and removed the bags filled with heroin, replacing it with the duffle bag of money. He put back the toilet and started to make his way out of the bathroom. All of a sudden, Gusto heard the loud sound of tires screeching. "What the fuck is that?", he thought as a feeling of panic came over him. As soon as he stepped foot out of the bathroom door, he saw FBI agents blitzing through the restaurant door, startling everyone. "Oh shit!", Gusto said. His heart dropped in to his stomach, and he froze, knowing he was caught red handed with no where to run. "Put your fucking hands up!" Two of the agents yelled aggressively with their guns drawn. Gusto swallowed hard, as he quickly put his hands in the air, letting his bags fall to the ground. Gusto dropped to his knees as the two agents rushed towards him. One of them grabbed Gusto by the back of his neck, squeezing it tightly before slamming his face to the ground. "Put your hands behind your back!", the other agent demanded before slapping the cuffs on Gusto. The agents grabbed Gusto by each arm, picking him up off the ground. A third agent stepped out of the crowd and made his way to the duffle bags on the floor, dropping down to one knee. He unzipped the bag to check the contents. "We got it", he stated with a sense of accomplishment. "I'll check inside the bathroom." The agent stood up and rushed to the bathroom, while the other two agents escorted Gusto outside. On his way out, Gusto spotted Neena standing near the counter watching the scene play out. He blew her a kiss and winked his eye, just to comfort her and to make her believe that everything was going to be okay.

CHAPTER 27: THEY GOT IT FOR THE LOW

Chameleon and Fonz were seated in a fast food restaurant in South Trenton. They ate their food as they recapped the move they just made. "I don't know baby, after robbing them for all that dope they might be dead broke", Chameleon stated. She was happy after she discovered the amount of dope they stole, and was somewhat surprised that Gusto and his crew was dealing with that much work. "You think so? Well there's only one way to find out", Fonz responded. He tried not to show it, but he was very pleased about their come up. It was one of the biggest stings he came across during his robbery career, and for that reason Fonz began feeling Chameleon even more. "All I have to do is go around my best friend. I know Geronimo corny ass gonna tell her everything that's going on." "Yeah, you do that", Fonz stated. "I'll do that, right after I do you. Shit, we deserve to treat each other to another sex session after this come up. Don't you think?", Chameleon asked with a lustful look in her eyes. Fonz still wanted to play it cool, and stick to the script. "Yeah, I guess we could do a little something. But first, we have to figure out how the hell we gonna get rid of all this shit. We have to be fast about it cause if that shit go bad we'll be out of luck with nothing", he explained. Chameleon went into deep thought for a moment, thinking about how they were going to solve the potential problem that was just brought to her attention. Suddenly, her eye brows raised. "Baby I know just how we gonna get rid of that shit. My peoples be out here moving dope. I'm sure he'll buy it off me." "Oh yeah, where at out here?" "Right on Center Street." "You think he around there right now?", Fonz asked. "Yup, him and the niggas he run with be out there all day long. And if he not, all I have to do is call him." "Alright then, lets go holla at ol' boy." Fonz thought about it for a few seconds. "Matter fact nah, I don't want none of them niggaz around there to see

141

my face or know that we're together." He remembered that he robbed a few dudes from that area, and didn't want anything to end up going wrong. "You don't think your peoples gonna try to do some bullshit, do you?" "Nah, he ain't gonna try no bullshit", she assured. "I'm gonna go to the hotel and grab a few bricks so I could.." Before she could finish her sentence, she noticed a beautiful dark skin little girl with long curly hair going down her back walk to the soda machine a few feet away with a small cup in her hand. "Aww she so pretty", Chameleon stated admiring the girl who she felt would resemble her daughter once she had a child. "Hurry up and look Fonz." Fonz turned his head and saw the little girl. "Ain't she pretty", Chameleon said smiling. "That's just how our baby gonna look", she looked at Fonz and waited to see how he was going to respond, but he didn't so she continued in a very innocent tone. "Baby, you gonna put a baby in me when we get our money right?" "Yeah you already know once our money right we can do whatever you want", he assured. Chameleon chuckled happily at the thought of having a baby girl by a full blooded goon like Fonz.

  After Chameleon finished her meal, she exited the fast food restaurant, jumped inside her car that was parked inside the parking lot, and drove straight to Center street. As soon as she turned down the street her eyes scanned both sides of the small block in search of her peoples. She spotted a crowd of young men, who all wore short sleeve white t-shirts, standing in front of a huge white house far down near the corner. "I know his ass probably right over there standing in the crowd", she thought as she slowly drove up on the crowd of men and rolled her driver window down. Immediately, all of the young men stopped what they were doing to get on point, not knowing what to expect from the tented out vehicle. "A yo, where Bobo at?", she asked in a high tone. When everyone saw Chameleon's beautiful chocolate face pop outside the window, they eased up.

"Hold on right quick, he in the house", a tall brown skin man with long corn rows standing by the porch stepped up. He walked up the porch steps, opened the front door, and stuck his head inside the house. "Yo Bobo, some chick out here want you." Bobo sat on the living room couch smoking a blunt while holding his cell phone in his hand sending someone a text message. Without saying a word, he got up from the couch and made his way to the front door. Once he stepped on the porch he saw that it was Chameleon a wide smile spread across his face. Chameleon returned the gesture. "Hurry up and get in the car. I got to tell you something real important", she said urgently. Without wasting any time, Bobo stepped off the porch. "Y'all hold this down until I come back", he stated looking at his crew before getting into the car.

"So what's up? What you doing popping up on me like this?", he asked wondering what was so important. Bobo was used to her calling before she stopped by. "Nah, it ain't like that. I would've called how I usually do, but I was in so much of a rush it slipped my mind", she explained without taking her eyes off the road. Despite the fact that Bobo was another one of Chameleon's fuck buddies from back in the day who hit her off with paper like everyone else, he was a certified dope boy that moved heroin like clock work and nine times out of ten would be interested in the undeniable deal Chameleon was about to throw at him. Bobo placed his hand on Chameleon's huge thigh and began gently rubbing it. "Aight now tell me what's so important you got to holla at me about", he stated trying to sound smooth. Chameleon smiled. "I got a whole bunch of dope for sale for real cheap." A surprised expression appeared on Bobo's face. Her having dope for sale was the last thing he expected to hear come out of her mouth. "Oh yeah. You got dope for sell huh. How cheap?", he asked curiously. "A hundred dollars a pack if you buying more than a hundred", she explained as she pulled over near the curb in front of a deli and parked. Bobo slightly jerked his head back as both of his eyebrows raised. "A hundred dollars a pack if I buy more than a hundred", he repeated the offer with a sense of disbelief and shock. Bobo chuckled, "Are you serious?" "Hell yeah I'm serious!", she shot back offended by his reaction. "When have you ever known me to play games when it come to money." "Yeah she do got a point there, but if she giving it out that cheap, it got to be some straight bullshit", Bobo thought to himself. "Yeah, you right. But I need to see how good the shit is before I even think about spending my money with you. Do you have a sample so I can test this shit out?" "Of course I do", she replied. Chameleon dug in her black Gucci purse that laid in between her thighs, and pulled out a blue and white pack of dope. "Here you go", she handed it to him. Bobo held the pack of dope up and looked at the stamp. It read *D-Boy Magic* in blue ink. "As soon as you have one of your fiends test it out, call me and let me know what's up", Chameleon told him. "You want me to drop you back off to the spot you was just at?", she said as she noticed a dark green Chrysler coming up in her rear view mirror. "Yeah", he responded. Once the vehicle rode pass, she pulled off right behind it. After Chameleon dropped Bobo off, she picked up Fonz from the fast food restaurant and told him how her meeting went with their potential customer.

144

Chapter 28: FAR FROM HOME

After driving around for almost 2 hours in the back seat of an unmarked car with his hands cuffed behind his back, Gusto's body became extremely cramped which annoyed him like crazy. "I wish these mu'fuckas would hurry up and get me to where I'm going", he said to himself squirming in the backseat trying to find a comfortable position. He looked at the two federal agents sitting in the front seats and sighed out loud obviously frustrated. "Damn man, what the fuck is taking so long?", he asked. Gusto began to wonder where they were taking him. He knew that anytime the Feds slammed cuffs on someone they would either take them to a county jail where they kept you until further notice, or to the Hudson County Jail. But from the looks of things they weren't headed in neither direction because they would've been there a long time ago. The FBI agent who sat in the passenger seat wearing black shades turned his head to look back at a frustrated Gusto. "Shut the fuck up", he barked in a high tone with a strong Spanish accent. "Fuck you", Gusto shot back. The FBI agent said something in Spanish to his partner who was driving, then looked back at Gusto and grinned wickedly. 15 minutes later, Gusto was still looking out of the backseat window, surveying the area curiously as they drove down an empty one way street occupied by an extremely huge dark grey 5 story building. It looked like an old ran down abandoned factory with chipped paint on it's walls.

Once they made it to the end of the street, they made a left turn, drove around the side of the building, and ended up in a huge empty parking lot. "What the fuck is we back here for", Gusto said to himself as a confused expression appeared on his face. He looked around and noticed a tall silver metal fence, which separated the parking lot from a small hill that led to a dirt road. It was so long you couldn't see the end of it. Suddenly, the driver stopped the car in the center of the parking lot and put the car in park. He turned to look back at Gusto, who still looked confused. "I want you to listen very carefully because this is only going to be a one shot deal", the federal agent stated seriously. "Do you understand me?" "Yeah I hear you", Gusto stated nonchalantly wondering what was about to roll off the agent's tongue. "Alright." The agent cleared his throat as his partner in the passenger seat turned to look back at Gusto with evil eyes. "You're not the one we want. We know that Flacko owns the restaurant and sells heroin out of it." Without taking his eyes off Gusto, he grabbed his tall black tape recorder out of his front pocket. "We'll let you go right here, and right now", he emphasized. "All you have to do is make a recorded statement saying that you were at the restaurant purchasing drugs from Flacko." The agent paused for a few seconds trying to get a read on Gusto but couldn't. "Once you do..." Before he could finish his sentence, Gusto frowned and responded harshly. "I ain't telling y'all shit. Get me the fuck from back here, and take me to whichever jail y'all gonna take me to. Fuck y'all think this is." The agent sitting in the passenger seat looked at his partner and yelled something in Spanish angrily. The other agent responded calmly also in Spanish without taking his eyes off of Gusto. He could tell Gusto really meant what he said, so he wasn't going to waste his time and ask again. The FBI agent in the passenger seat climbed out of the vehicle and opened the back door. Confused and lost for words, Gusto slowly climbed out of the backseat, struggling with his hands cuffed behind his back. Once he was out of the car, the federal agent slammed the door closed, and climbed back into the driver's seat. The car sped off, making a left turn to go out the parking lot, leaving Gusto standing in the middle of the vacant parking lot with his hands cuffed behind his back looking stupid. "What the fuck type of shit is this", he thought. An awkward feeling came over his as he began to think why in the hell would the feds drop him off in the back of an abandoned building after catching him red handed with a huge amount of heroin and money. He just stood there for a few seconds and then sighed in relief and exclaimed, "Man let me hurry up and get from back here before they come back or some shit." He made his way from behind the huge building and up the empty dead end street.

Gusto didn't know where he was, but he damn sure knew he had to find someone to help him get the tight handcuffs from off his wrist. He needed his hands free so he could grab his cell phone from his pocket. For a good twenty minutes, Gusto walked through different blocks in search of some help. He finally spotted a few people far down on the corner of the long street he was on. As he approached the corner he looked up at the street sign, it read Bloomfield Ave. He knew he was definitely in the hood. "One of these mu'fuckas gotta help me", he said to himself as he noticed a husky brown skin young man strolling towards him. "A yo bro. I need your help", Gusto stated eagerly as he approached the young man, damn near knocking him over. The young man stopped in his tracks and quickly motioned his hand to prevent Gusto from running in to him. "Calm down bro. You aight? What happened?", he asked with raised eye brows. "Can you help me get these handcuffs off", Gusto asked desperately before he turned and showed him his cuffed wrists. "Oh shit, you just ran from the police", the young man exclaimed in shock, looking around to see if the stranger was still being chased. "It's a long story", Gusto shot back urgently. "Can you please just help me get these shits off my wrist?" The young man looked around again and then said, "Yeah, I got you man. Follow me over here." The young man turned around, walked a few feet up the block, and then cut in between two houses. "Alright now listen, turn around and hold your hands out as far away from your back as you can", he instructed looking at Gusto dead in the face as he

147

pulled a 38 revolver from his waist. Without saying a word, Gusto did exactly what he was told. "Man I hope this nigga don't make a mistake and shoot me." The young man was holding the barrel of the gun directly on the small metal piece connected to both of the cuffs. BLOW! The young man pulled the trigger, and the hot slug pierced the metal piece splitting it in half. Gusto quickly turned around and lifted his arm in the air, stretching them out. "Aww man. Good looking bro", Gusto thanked him, now feeling relieved. "I've been in those tight ass cuffs for like 4 hours straight." "That shit ain't about nothing. Real niggas do real things", the young man replied plainly as he tucked his gun back on his hip. Immediately Gusto grabbed his cell to call Geronimo, but the battery died after the first ring. "Damn!", he exclaimed in frustration. He tried to turn the cell phone back on but it turned right back off. He didn't know Geronimo's number by heart or anyone elses. "A yo big bro my battery dead, can I use your phone to call me a cab?", he asked remembering he still had his cab fair in his pocket. "Yeah, I got you." The man handed Gusto the phone. "You can at least tell me ya name and what happened." The young man was shocked to hear such an absurd story and gave him his input on the situation.
Once the cab arrived, Gusto was finally on his way home back to Trenton. He got dropped of on Fountain Ave, where he ran into Geronimo and told him about the unbelievable story.

CHAPTER 29: WHAT'S BEEF

Itty Bitty and Talk Slick was having a real life two-man crack party inside Talk Slick's filthy upstairs bedroom. There were dirty shoes and clothes all over the dresser, and other junk piled up on the floor. The windows and door were closed so the two men were taking in all the foul odor of funk and crack smoke that lingered throughout the air. Talk Slick and Itty Bitty sat on the edge of the bed watching Sanford and Son. Talk Slick put his crack pipe in his mouth and struck his green lighter with his crusty thumb, causing a large flame to appear. He held it up to the opposite end of the stem where the boulder of crack sat, and sucked. Once he was finished, he removed the crack pipe from his mouth and exhaled slowly, grey smoke rose into the air. 'Boy this gone be some good shit I tell ya, cause I'm higher than a mufucka", he stated with droopy eyes as his words dragged. Between the both of them, Talk Slick and Itty Bitty had smoked at least eighteen grams of crack so he definitely was feeling it. "Awww, man you high already", Itty Bitty exclaimed as he looked at him with wide eyes. He was high too, he just wasn't as high as Talk Slick.

The two never really got high together but out of now where Itty Bitty offered him a free smoke out and promised that everything would be on him. A lazy smile spread across Talk Slick face. "What 'chu talking about man? We smoke damn near a ounce in this bitch." "Yeah I got his ass right where I want him", Itty Bitty thought deviously laughing to himself. "Nah, man. I'm just fucking with you", Itty Bitty stated before he let out a fake laugh, revealing his yellow teeth. He slapped the palm of his hand on his thigh. "I was about to say what the fuck you be doing taking ounces of crack to the head or some shit", Talk Slick stated sounding slow and high. As soon as Talk Slick turned his head and focused back on the television, Itty Bitty discretely pulled a hammer out of his front pants pocket and

whacked Talk Slick in the head with all his might.
"Aggghhh", Talk Slick yelled in agony. His head split open
instantly as he slid of the bed and fell to the ground. He
quickly clutched the bloody gash in his head with both
hands. Blood poured all over the mess on the floor.
"Aaaagggghhhh!", he yelled again as an excruciating pain
began pulsating in his head "You thought you was just
gonna get away with punching me in the mouth ,didn't
you? Shut the fuck up!", Itty Bitty growled with clinched
teeth as he quickly got up from the edge of the bed leaned
down and cracked him in the head with the hammer again.
THUMP! Talk Slick scull split open and globs of blood
began to squirt out. His entire body twitched uncontrollably
for a few seconds before it went stiff. Itty Bitty cocked his
arm back and was about to strike him a gain but stopped
when he realized Talk Slick was no longer moving. That's
when Itty Bitty started to panic. "Oh shit. This nigga
dead!", he exclaimed with raised eye brows breathing
heavily while looking down at Talk Slick's lifeless body. Itty
Bitty turned around, grabbed all of his belongings from off
the bed, wiped the door knob off with the bottom of his
shirt, and rushed out the room. Thinking about getting
caught caused the inside of his stomach to tighten as he
nervously rushed down the stairs. Without even realizing it,
he dropped the bloody hammer at the bottom of the stairs.
Itty decided not to leave out the front door just in case
somebody was watching, so he darted out the back door.

      Meanwhile, Gusto sat on the porch steps of his house
on Sweats Ave replaying everything that took place in the
last few days. He felt dumb as a box of rocks and had a
pitiful look on his face. He figured out that the so called
feds where men under Flocko's drug team, and they just
used the F.B.I. stunt to throw everyone in the restaurant off
from realizing that a kidnapping and robbery was
transpiring. He didn't understand why, at first. Knowing
Flocko had enough money to last him three life times. But

then it dawned on him, Flocko was a very strict business man who had zero tolerance for bullshit. It was only a matter of time before Gusto had to pay for his senseless mistake in shorting Flocko when it came to his money. Flocko took Gusto's short comings as disrespect, therefore he pressed the delete button on him as soon as he felt the time was right. His exact orders was, "Let him live if he's a stand up guy but kill him if he's a low down rat that can't handle the consequences of his actions." "Damn man. I need something to smoke", Gusto said to himself. Gusto was broke as a joke, and only had twenty dollars to his name. He lost his dope and coke connect so it was going to be damn near impossible to get to his king pin status again. Gusto wanted to suggest that Geronimo purchase coke from his cousin Butchy, but he decided to wait and see what kind of solution Geronimo would come up with first. He figured since Lango had plugged him in with Flocko, he would eventually find out about the mishap and cut all ties with him as well. Gusto got up from off the steps, and began walking down the street. Once he made it to the corner of Sweets Ave and the boulevard, he saw a crippled Chopo sitting on the hood of a white Pontiac. "Damn, lil bro all fucked up in the game", he thought to himself knowing Chopo's physical conditions was mainly because of him. "What's good Chopo. You aight?', Gusto greeted. Chopo had on a white short sleeve t shirt that had RIP Little Petey on it in big bold letters with a picture of the both of them standing side by side holding wads of cash in their hands. "What up bro", Chopo replied sounding depressed. Lil Petey's funeral was just the other day, so he was still fucked up in the head. He also finally faced the fact that his arm was dead and his hip bone was shattered, which caused him to walk slow and very deformed. Chopo's injuries caused him to be incapable of avenging his best friends death. "What you doing out here?", Gusto asked. "Don't you think you should be in the house letting your body rest?" "Man

I'm tired of staying in the house. I needed to get some fresh air", Chopo shot back with a hint of frustration in his tone. "Plus it's no reason to let it rest. Im stuck like this forever." Gusto took a deep breath as he looked in Chopo's face and could tell he was going through hell. He placed his hand on Chopo's shoulder, and lowered his head looking him dead in the eyes. "Listen lil bro, don't even trip about that shit that went down. It's going to get handled, trust me", he assured seriously. Without saying a word, Chopo just stood there staring back at Gusto. Gusto didn't know how to take his silence so he continued. "You heard?" Chopo nodded his head and said, "Yeah." "I'll be right back, I'm about to go in the store and buy some black & milds real quick."

As Gusto approached the store, he noticed Lango's hot orange custom made Corvette parked on the corner. "Oh they really think shit sweet huh", he thought to himself as his adrenaline began to rush, knowing he had the drop on his enemies. Without wasting a second, he darted across the street running as fast as he could to Talk Slick's house to grab the black glock 40 caliber hand gun he stashed. Gusto hurriedly grabbed his key out of his front pants pocket, opened the door, and rushed inside the house. He quickly removed the cushions on the couch where he hid the pistol and became extremely angry when he realized it was no longer there. "Fuck! Man this some bullshit", he grumbled. Gusto began pacing back and forth, starring at the floor trying to come up with an idea. Suddenly, he noticed a hammer laying on the floor near the steps. He darted to pick it up, and was so focused on retaliating that he didn't even notice the blood smeared all over it. Gusto went in to the kitchen and grabbed a butcher knife out of the dish holder. "Fuck that. I'm about to put these shits to work!", he growled. After experiencing all the drama within the past few months, he was so emotionally off balance that he didn't give a fuck how things would turn out. He was going to walk right up on Lango, stab him and beat him to death with the hammer in front of whoever was standing on the block. Gusto made it out of the kitchen and into the living room. Just then, the front door was kicked opened. DOOM! The door swung open, crashing against the wall, making way for the swarm of Trenton police officers to rush inside. Their guns were drawn right on Gusto. "Put your fucking weapons down", the officers yelled aggressively in unison, slowly stepping towards Gusto. Gusto's quickly dropped his weapons and put his hands in the air. He knew this wasn't no scheme because he recognized the local cops faces. One of the officers rushed Gusto, put his hands behind his back, and slammed the cuffs on him. All the other cops scattered every where and began flipping the house up side down. Some of them rushed upstairs and some of them darted into the kitchen and basement. "Y'all ain't doing nothing but wasting y'all time because it ain't nothing in here", Gusto exclaimed cockily, knowing there wasn't no drugs in the house. Gusto looked at the sergeant standing a few feet away and smirked. "Shut the fuck up!", the sergeant barked, raising his voice. "Who told you to talk." He looked at the officer that held Gusto's arm. "If he says anything else, knock his fucking teeth out of his mouth." One of the police officers upstairs rushed to the edge of the steps and yelled out urgently, "Sergeant we found a dead body up here." Sergeant Larkon's eyes grew wide in shock. "It's a dead body up there!", he exclaimed in disbelief noticing the baffled look that appeared on Gusto's face. He quickly rushed to the bottom of the steps. "Are you sure the person is dead?", he asked looking up at the officer on the top of the stairs. "Yes sir", he replied in a high tone. "Alright, listen, don't touch nothing else up there and tell all the officers to come down stairs", Sergeant Larkon commanded in a high tone before turning around to look at Gusto. "I thought we weren't going to find anything you dip shit", he stated with a hint of sarcasm. The Narcs had Gusto under surveillance for the last few days and was raiding the house in search of drugs, they didn't expect to discover a dead body. Gusto just stood their speechless with a dumbfounded look on his face, wondering who's body was upstairs. "Go throw his ass in one of the cars outside", the sergeant barked. The officer escorted Gusto out the house.

CHAPTER 30: REDRUM

Almost everyone in the city was talking about Gusto and the unfortunate incident he just got caught up in. Geronimo and Shaky sat on the couch in her house talking about his arrest. Chameleon was also there listening attentively, adding her two cents every now and then. "I still can't believe Gusto locked up for killing poor old Talk Slick. That's crazy", Shaky said with a hint of doubt in her tone. "Well shit, Talk Slick probably owed him some money or something", Chameleon exclaimed. "Man Gusto ain't do that shit", Geronimo shot back twisting his face up. He knew Gusto like the back of his hand and felt in his heart that Gusto would never stoop so low and kill Talk Slick, especially with a hammer. If anything he would've just shot him. Geronimo also would've known first hand if the two had any problems with each other. "How the hell you know if he did it or not?", Chameleon shot back defiantly. "What you was there or something?" Geronimo paused for a split second, and then responded sounding a little agitated. "Nah, I wasn't there. But I know that nigga like the back of my hand." "So what's that supposed to mean?", she asked with raised eyebrows as she quickly jerked her neck to the side. "It mean I know he wouldn't do no shit like that. That's what it mean", he told her with an attitude. Chameleon could tell she had Geronimo all worked up and began laughing sarcastically. "Well shit, his money long. He'll bail out." She waited eagerly to hear Geronimo's response to determine whether or not they still had cash on deck. Geronimo just stared at her with an angry expression on his face. "This cold hearted whore bitch need to be dealt with", he thought to himself. Shaky looked at Geronimo and could tell he was on fire. "Baby just chill out", she told him as she gently rubbed her small manicured hand across his broad chest. She looked at Chameleon. "Damn girl. I know you're gonna go visit him to find out what's going on." Chameleon looked at Shaky like she lost her mind. "I ain't going to go see him. He ain't my man. He better call his baby mom." Chameleon found out Tayla had her baby several months ago.

The cordless phone began to ring. RING! RING! RING! Shaky quickly leaned forward to grab it. "Hello", she stated. The automated operator began talking. "This is Bell Atlantic Phone Services. You have a collect call from... Gusto..an inmate in the Mercer County Correctional Center..." "Oh shit, this Gusto right here", Shaky exclaimed, and quickly handed the phone to Geronimo. He listened to the instructions before accepting the call. "What's good my nigga", Geronimo stated animatedly. Immediately Gusto recognized his right hand man voice and sighed deeply. "Many they got me in here on some straight up bullshit." "Yeah, man I know", Geronimo agreed as he glanced at both females and noticed they were all in his mouth. "How those people coming?" "I don't really want to get into it over the phone but just to set the record straight, I ain't do this dumb shit they charged me with bro", Gusto explained. "I pretty much figured that", Geronimo assured. "But anyway, my bail is a half a million cash or bond. I already talked to the bail bond. They said they only want fifteen thousand and six co-signers", Gusto informed. "Word up? That's all they want for half a million dollar bail?" "Yeah man, that's all they want", Gusto stated before he paused for a few seconds, then continued. "Listen man, you already know what happened after I went to bust that move in Paterson, I ain't got a fucking dollar to my name. I need you to pop this punk ass bail for me my nigga. I know you got a nice piece of change put up." Geronimo swallowed hard, knowing he only had ten thousand tucked in the stash. He was blowing all the fast money they were making thinking shit was going to last forever, not to mention the losses he took recently. "I got majority of it. I'm gonna see if Chopo could come up with the rest." "Damn,

156

he ain't even got fifteen thousand put up", Gusto thought to himself in disappointment. "Aight man, go find that lil nigga right now and see what's up. I gotta get the fuck out of here", Gusto told him. "Don't even trip, I'm about to go find Chopo right now. Call me in a few days, everything should be put together by then. Hold your head." After the two hung up, Geronimo stood up from the couch and was on his way out. "I'll be right back." He then felt his cell phone vibrating. "Who the fuck is this", he thought before putting his cell phone to his ear. "Yo what's good." "What up bro, this Bubby. I gotta holla at you about some real important shit. Where you at?" "I'm on Fountain." "Alright, I'll be there in twenty minutes." After the two hung up, Geronimo walked out the front door.

After getting off the phone with Geronimo, Gusto went straight to his three bunk cell and sat on the shiny metal stool that was connected to a desk. "What the fuck man", Gusto said to himself. He was stressed out of his mind, there were too many negative emotions torturing his inner being. It felt like his body was about to give up on him. Gusto felt like he was trapped in an everlasting nightmare he couldn't wake up from. He couldn't believe after all the shit he'd been through he was now was sitting in the county jail facing forever for a murder he didn't commit. He couldn't sleep at all and stayed up the night before trying to figure out how the hell he was going to get out of this fucked up situation. Gusto broke out of his daze when he heard the cell door open. It was his bunky, who was standing by the doorway holding a steaming hot cup of coffee in his hand. "What's up bunky, you aight?", he asked in a concerned tone, slowly closing the door behind him. "Yeah, I'm good. I guess", Gusto replied dryly. "Well my name Redrum and I'm from Atlantic City." Redrum introduced himself as he leaned forward and extended his hand for a handshake.

Redrum was a light skin black man with slanted eyes, skinny bright pink lips, and long wet looking hair that stopped at his shoulders. "My name Gusto. I'm from out here." The two slapped hands. Redrum was sleep when Gusto came in last night so the two never got the chance to kick it until now. Gusto noticed the way Redrum's hair was slicked back like he had a perm in it, and assumed that he was a pimp, especially knowing that type of activity went on heavy in Atlantic City. "What you some type of pimp or something?", Gusto asked bluntly. Redrum began laughing. "Yeah, I be pimping. What made you ask me that?" "I don't know. Just from the way you got your hair and where you from, I guess. How you end up getting locked-up up here though?" "Man, fucking around with my bottom bitch and one of my other hoes. I ended up bringing them up here to handle something and got into some unnecessary bullshit", he told him not really wanting to talk about his case. "My bail three hundred thousand cash or bond. I'm trying to pop that thang though. I got seven of my hoes working on it now." "Oh yeah", Gusto stated. "Damn, he must be locked up for some serious shit", Gusto thought. "Well shit, you in a better position than me. My bail is half a million and I'm locked up for a fucking murder that I didn't even do nor knew about", Gusto explained with a hint of depression is his tone. A surprised expression appeared on Redrum's face. "Damn that's fucked up. You ain't go the money to bail out?" "Yeah, I got most of it, my man getting the rest up right now, so I should be good", Gusto stated. Redrum nodded his head and took a sip from his smoking hot cup of coffee. "That's what's up. You should be good then." "Yeah, I hope", Gusto stated as he slowly ran his hand over the top of his head. "They want fifteen stacks, and all I need is a few more." "Which bail bondsmen you using", Redrum asked curiously. "A-A Bail Bondsmen. They office by the police station out east Trenton. Redrum paused for a few seconds before he responded. "They expensive as hell out here. I'm using a bail bonds from out my way." Suddenly Gusto thought he heard someone calling his last name out in the day space. "A yo you heard that? It sound like somebody just called me." "Nah, I ain't here nothing", Redrum stated. "Let's go see what's up though."

Gusto stood up and the both of them exited the cell and strolled into the day space. Several inmates were seated at metal tables playing board games while others were watching T.V. near the steps. Redrum spotted a tall dark skin correctional officer standing across the room. "A yo C .O. you called my bunky?" "Yeah, he has an attorney visit in the quiet room", the officer replied. "Let me go see what this dumb ass public defender talking about", Gusto stated as he looked at Redrum. He made his way to the C.O.'s desk. "Go inside, he's already in there waiting for you." The officer stepped aside to allow Gusto to get pass. Gusto looked through the huge glass window and saw his public defender. He was sitting at a small wooden table behind a metal fence that was meant to be a partition. Gusto stepped inside the small room, and sat in a plastic burgundy chair a few feet away from the metal cage. He made sure to make eye contact with the public defender. "How are you Mr. Anderson. I'm Jonathan Murphy from the Public Defender's Office", Mr. Murphy explained as he politely clutched a folder in his hand. He was a chubby West Indian man with a light goatee, and straight jet black hair that was slicked back. The grey suit he wore was wrinkled, so it looked cheap. "Listen man, they got me in here on some straight up bullshit", Gusto was talking with his hands. "I really didn't do the crime I'm charged with. What kind of evidence they got and can you get my bail lowered?" "Hold on Mr. Anderson, slow down", Mr. Murphy stated as he too motioned with his hands. "Man what kind of evidence they got", Gusto blurted out disregarding what was just said to him. "It can't be much because I ain't do the shit." "Listen Mr. Anderson, in order to find out all the evidence they have, we're going to have to get your discoveries. From what I heard, they have the murder weapon with your finger prints all over it." "They what?", Gusto was in disbelief. "Yes, they said the elderly man was beat to death with a hammer", Mr. Murphy continued to explain. "Oh shit the hammer", Gusto's eyes grew wide. He sighed deeply and hung his head low, rubbing his palms across the top of his head. His mind flashed back to the scene when he picked up the weapon from off the living room floor. Mr. Murphy could tell by Gusto's body language that there was some truth to the story. Gusto lifted his head up. "So can you at least get my bail lowered", he asked desperately. "Ummm, I highly doubt it", Mr. Murphy replied putting emphasis on his words. "But anyhow Mr. Anderson, can you please sign this paper that states you're willing to pay the thirty dollar fee to have me represent you for this case." He leaned forward and made an attempt to pass Gusto a white sheet of paper through the slot in the middle of the fence. Gusto frowned at the paper. "I ain't signing that shit! You can't even get my fucking bail dropped!" Gusto stood up from his seat, and stormed out of the quiet room.

While walking back to his cell, Gusto noticed Redrum standing near the shower talking to a husky brown skin man with a bald head. Once Gusto made it to his cell, he jumped straight in the middle bunk and started thinking about his fucked up situation all over again. Seconds later, the cell door swung up. Redrum stepped inside the cell, closing the door behind him. "What's up Gusto. You aight?" "Yeah I'm good. That dumb ass public defender got on my nerves a little bit." "Who was the dude you was talking to by the shower?" "Oh, umm, that was one of my niggas from my city", Redrum said with raised eyebrows. "I just came to make sure you was good. "I'm about to go back out there and finish hollering at him. If you get hungry it's plenty of food under the bunk. Help yourself", Redrum stated as he exited the cell. Gusto just laid there, he wondered why Redrum and the boy from his town wasn't in the same room together.

CHAPTER 31: CAUGHT IN THE ACT

Geronimo stood on the corner of Fountain Ave and the Boulevard, across the street from a corner store. He called Chopo a few minutes ago and told him where to meet up so he could tell him what was going on. He was also waiting for Bubby to come through the hood, that way he could find out what he had to tell him that was so important. Geronimo spotted Itty Bitty a few houses down walking towards him eating out of a white platter filled with smelly pig feet. "Damn Itty Bitty just popped up out of no where. He must've just came from the side of one of those houses", he thought to himself. Itty Bitty finally reached Geronimo. "I heard what happened. Is my boy alright?", he stated. "Yeah he good. I'm getting the money for his bail right now. He'll be out soon, that shit ain't about nothing", Geronimo told him "That's what's up", Itty Bitty replied with raised eyebrows. "When I read it in the paper I said to myself, Talk Slick must've really did some real live bullshit for Gusto to do that to him." "He said he didn't do it", Geronimo stated. "Well shit, if he ain't do it who the hell did? I know somebody had to see something", Itty Bitty still trying to feel Geronimo out. "From my understanding nobody ain't see nothing. Matter fact, where the hell you was at yesterday?", Geronimo stated with a hint of suspicion in his tone. "Hell if I know, I be too high to remember what I did an hour ago. "I'm gonna holler at you", Itty Bitty stepped off and began strolling down the street. "Itty Bitty black ass shot the hell out", Geronimo thought to himself shaking his head as he watched Itty Bitty speed walk down the Boulevard. "What's up", Chopo exclaimed in a high tone as he approached Geronimo from the opposite side. Geronimo jumped, Chopo caught him off guard. "Oh shit bro. I ain't even seen you." "What's up. I heard about what happened to Gusto. That's what you called me down here for ain't it?" "Yeah. He trying to bail out, but he short five stacks. I know you got that stashed some where", Geronimo stated. "Man, I ain't got no five thousand dollars", Chopo shot back with a hint of resentment in his tone. "I just helped Lil Petey's mom pay for his funeral by myself." Geronimo tightened his face, breathing heavily out of his nose. "Damn bro, you can at least give up something." Chopo sighed as he looked away for a split second. "All that money this nigga was out here getting, you mean to tell me he can't post his bail", Chopo thought to himself. Chopo was never told about any of the losses the team took, so he didn't know Gusto really was assed out. "Aight man. I got twenty five hundred for him", Chopo sounded like he really didn't want to give up the cash. "Aight, where is it?", Geronimo asked urgently as he noticed Bubby's all black tented out Intrepid parking across the street. "Matter fact, wait here. I'm about to ask Bubby if he can take you to your crib to grab it". Geronimo made his way across the street towards Bubby's car.

Geronimo climbed inside of the car to speak with Bubby. "What's good bro. What you…". Bubby interrupted, "Take a good look at this shit." He pulled a pack of heroin out of his front pants pocket and tossed it on Geronimo's lap. Geronimo held it up in order to examine it. "Where the hell you get this shit from?", he questioned in anger and shock. Geronimo noticed the stamp on the pack of heroin was the exact same stamp from the batch that was stolen. At that moment, a feeling of pure rage shot though Geronimo's chest. "My little cousin Rell from out South Trenton said some bad ass dark skin chick with slanted eyes and a big ass be coming out there breaking them niggas off with dirt cheap prices", Bubby explained. Gusto told him their stash had been stolen a few weeks ago, Bubby also knew they was the only people in town that had the same dope stamp. Without saying a word, Geronimo just stared at Bubby, knowing exactly what he was trying to insinuate. His mind began racing a hundred miles an hour. "Shaky said she never told Chameleon, so how the fuck she knew where the stash was at", he asked himself silently not wanting to believe the fact that his girl lied to him. Geronimo squinted his eyes. "Oh yeah that slime ball bitch crazy", he stated with a hint of suspicion in his tone. "Take me out South Trenton to go holla at your cousin. I need to hear it out his own mouth before I let Gusto know what's up." He really wanted to be face to face to get a read on him, and see if this was some sort of scandalous game. "Aight, we about to shoot out there right now then", Bubby stated plainly. Bubby took the car out of park and was about to pull off, Geronimo had almost forgot about Chopo. "Oh shit! I need you to take Chopo to his crib real quick so he could grab a few stacks for Gusto's bail." "Gusto locked up?", Bubby surprised eyes grew wide. "Hell yeah he locked up. You don't read the newspaper?" Geronimo looked at Bubby like he was crazy. "What he locked up for?" "For a body, you got something for his bail?", Geronimo asked. "Umm my money funny right now. I'll probably be able to put something together in a few days", Bubby told him. Geronimo sighed as he shook his head. "Tight ass niggas always crying broke", he thought to himself. Knowing Bubby had a few dollars to spare. "Man beep the horn so Chop can get in the car", he demanded with a hint of hostility in his tone, motioning his hands towards Chopo, who was still standing across the street Bubby beeped the horn and Chopo got inside the backseat of the car.

Once Bubby took Chopo to pick up the money, he drove to the south side of Trenton. "A yo man, don't you think you should've called him to let him know you was on your way", Geronimo stated. "Nah, I ain't gotta call him. They be out here all day long moving that smack", Bubby assured as he turned down Center Street. Geronimo began surveying both sides of the slightly empty streets while the car slowly drove down. "Man it's dead as a mu'fucking

164

cemetery out here." "Cool out, they probably on the other end of the street in the alleyway or something", Bubby told him as he gently pressed his foot on the brake. Two young brown skin boys were playing in the street, squirting each other with colorful water guns. "Now look at these two little mu'fuckas. Where the hell they parents at?", Geronimo was getting frustrated. BEEP! BEEP! BEEP! Bubby beeped the car horn startling the kids. As Bubby began driving down the street, Geronimo's eyes grew wide as if they were going to pop out of his head. "Oh shit Bubby. There go that bitch right there", he pointed at Chameleon. She was walking out of a house with a black gym bag in her hand, and got in to a black car with black tents. "I told you my cousin said it was some dark skin broad with slanted eyes. She must have just finished serving them in the house. That's they spot she just came out of ", Bubby stated. "Follow that piece of shit bitch and find out where the hell she going!", Geronimo ordered. Without saying a word, Bubby did just that.

Chameleon drove down the street and made a left turn. Their vehicle's were a nice distance away so she never noticed Bubby's car behind her. Once Bubby and Geronimo swung around the corner, they saw her car stop in front of the deli. They noticed a very familiar looking man exit the deli and walk up to the car. "Aint that Fonz crazy ass?", Geronimo couldn't believe it. He kept his eyes on Fonz who was getting inside Chameleon's car. The two knew who Fonz was, and was well aware of his notorious reputation as a murderous stick up kid. "Yeah that's him", Bubby responded. "What you want me to do? Pull up on the side of the car?" "Hell no! Matter fact, stop the car", Geronimo was shook up in a complete state of shock. He didn't know what exactly was going on, but he knew what Fonz crazy ass was about, and choked up. Chameleon and Fonz pulled off, driving down the street. "So what you want me to do now?", Bubby asked. Geronimo was captured by his

165

thoughts so he couldn't respond right away. "Take me back out the way. This shit crazy." Bubby bust a quick U-turn and headed back towards North Trenton.

CHAPTER 32: CHECK MATE

Gusto and Redrum had been in their cell for the last two hours playing chess. The two of them quietly concentrated on the chess board. Gusto played the white pieces and only had four pawns and a king left while Redrum had more than half of his black army still standing strong. "Check!", Redrum exclaimed as he moved his queen, cornering Gusto's king. Gusto had already lost every game so far, and became frustrated after his opponent's move. He felt his best move would be to move his king closer to his pawns. A wide grin slowly crept across Redrum's face. He moved his Bishop from across the board, closing Gusto's king in completely. "Mate!", he yelled proudly. Gusto surveyed the board trying to find an opening but realized he was doomed. "Damn man!" Redrum started to chuckle as he cleaned the board. "I'm good. I don't want to play no more. I'm tired of getting my ass whooped and I'm tired of standing up", Gusto had to admit. He walked to the bottom bunk. "Is it alright if I sit on your bed?", he asked looking down at Redrum's neatly made up bed. "Yeah, go head", Redrum told him while picking up the chess pieces from off the desk and placing them in a clear plastic bag. When Gusto sat on the bed he looked up and noticed several pictures stuck to the bottom of the second bunk. "Oh shit, you ain't tell me you had pictures. Can I check them out?" "Yeah, go head." Gusto leaned back and surveyed all the pictures and noticed they were all photographs of the same pretty Spanish female with a voluptuous body. "Damn. No disrespect, but ol' girl bad as hell." Every last one of his pictures were of her, so he knew it had to be his main bitch, or close to it. Gusto sat back up and looked at Redrum. "Let me find out you slipping on your pimping and she got you sprung the fuck out." Redrum burst into a loud laughter. "Nah, never that, that 's my bottom broad", he stated smoothly. "She keep all my other hoes in check and make sure everything that need to be taken care of get taken care of while I'm in here." "That's your bottom broad?" Gusto was so surprised, he couldn't believe a girl so pretty would be ripping and running in the streets selling herself. "Man a nigga see her and will wife her real quick." Redrum chuckled again, "Yeah, she is sexy as fuck. She be bringing in that paper too. That's why I'm so surprised she taking so long to pop my bail." Gusto got up quickly from the bed. "You just made me remember I have to call my peoples and find out what's going on with my bail."

Gusto picked up the first phone available, and called Geronimo. It didn't take long for Geronimo to accept the call. "What's good my nigga", Gusto greeted cheerfully. "Man you ain't going to believe this shit I'm about to tell you", Geronimo stated dramatically getting straight to the point. "What?" "I found out who stole our work out the trunk", Geronimo replied. "Who?" "Ya slime ball ass girl." Gusto twisted his face up. "How the hell you know that?", he had a hint of doubt in his tone. "Because her sneaky ass be out South Trenton damn near giving it away like it's free or something. One of our peoples got wind of it and hit me up. I saw her with my own eyes. She was coming out of one of those little niggas spot with a gym bag." "Why the fuck you ain't do something?" "Because man, she was with that crazy ass stick up kid Fonz", Geronimo informed. A puzzled look appeared on Gusto's face. "What the fuck was she doing with him?" "I don't know man, but that's who she was with. And I wasn't trying to run up on that nigga. You already know how he is." "Man this pussy ass nigga", Gusto mumbled under his breath. Gusto was well aware of Fonz's reputation for being a cold blooded killer, but he was tired of Geronimo always bitching out. Without saying a word, he listed to Geronimo talk and quickly began to analyze everything. "Chameleon stanking ass got this coo-coo crazy ass stick up nigga rolling with her while she riding around making money selling my shit", Gusto thought. Not only was it hard for him to digest his main lady's unexpected betrayal, but he also found it hard to put the rest of the puzzle pieces together. He knew Geronimo wasn't making this up, but it still didn't add up. Suddenly, it clicked and hit him like a ton of bricks. "She fucking that nigga and bought him in on the scheme", Gusto thought trying to keep his composure. His entire body heated up and his heart was full of pure rage. He was so emotionally and mentally disturbed, he no longer wanted to hear or talk about the incident. He just wanted to hurry up and get home so he could handle it. "Alright bro, just fall back until I get home. What's up with the bail money?" Geronimo sighed before answering, "Chopo hit me off with like two stacks, so I only need like three more. I hollered at our so called fly boys, but they said they were fucked up and been loosing out on a whole lot of money since our ship started sinking. Oh yeah, Bubby did say he was going to try to put something together for you, just give him a few days." "Them pretty ass niggas ain't got a few hundred dollars a piece", Gusto's mind was racing. "Aight, listen man. I'ma call the bail bond and see if they can take that twelve thousand you got right now, and allow me to give the remaining three to them once I'm home. I'll call you later on to let you know what's up." "Aight bro, stay up", Geronimo stated before the two hung up. Gusto dialed the number to ABC bail bond but when no one answered the phone, he decided to go back to his cell where he could digest what was just told to him.

Redrum was sitting on the stool connected to the desk eating a huge honey bun watching Gusto as he walked in to the cell. He could tell Gusto was upset. "Damn some bullshit must have happened with his money or something", Redrum thought to himself. Gusto climbed slowly into the second bunk and just laid there on his back looking up at the ceiling. It was very quiet in the cell for several seconds

169

before Redrum finally decided to break the silence. "What's good? You aight?" "Yeah, I'm good", Gusto replied dryly avoiding eye contact. "You sure, cause it seem like you kind of upset." Gusto breathed heavily out his nose, as he asked himself whether or not should he talk to Redrum about what he was going through. "Fuck it, he ain't from my town and ain't going to know who I'm talking about anyway." Gusto turned to look at Redrum. "I just found out my main lady whacked me for all my work." Redrum's eyes grew wide. "Damn! Word up? That's some straight up bullshit." "Yeah, I know. It's all good though. Karma is a mu'fucka." "So you still going to be able to bail out right?", Redrum asked. "Hell yeah, I still should be able to bail out. My right hand man holding that paper for me. The only problem is that it's kind of hard to scrape the rest of the money. I'll wait for like another thirty minutes before I call the bail bond and try to talk him into taking this twelve thousand I got right now, and then let me pay the rest as soon as I come home." "Like I already tried to tell you, I know a bail bond that will take that twelve thousand right now with no problem", Redrum told him. "You probably only need like two co-signers." "Oh yeah", Gusto remembered Redrum mentioning it last night. "I'll see what my man is talking about first. If they not fucking with me, and if my man's can't come up with the rest of the bread, I'll call your man." Redrum thought for a few seconds. "Alright, if it's ok with you I'm about to call my peoples and tell her to get at the bail bond in advance, just in case shit don't go right. Ya dig." Redrum exited the room to go make his phone call. Gusto waited the 30 minutes before reaching back out to the bail bond. This time someone answered the phone, but Gusto's request was denied. His options were getting slim, it was either wait to see if Geronimo could come up with the rest of the money, or go with Redrum's connect in Atlantic City. Either way he knew something had to give, and the time was now.

CHAPTER 33: VIDEO PHONE

Shaky had just got out of the shower and slipped in to her all white cotton bathrobe. She sat on the edge of her neatly made bed holding the tv remote in her hand, flicking through the channels. Shaky was still waiting on Geronimo to come over, it's been five days since she seen him and her voluptuous body was yearning for his touch. "Where the fuck this nigga at? He better not be with another bitch", she thought to herself. "I'm about to get me some cookies and cream ice cream." Shaky sat the remote down and left out the bedroom. Once downstairs, she noticed Chameleon forgot to turn off the lights before leaving out of the house with Fonz. She went in to the living room area to turn of the lamp and spotted Chameleon's cellphone on the laying on the couch. "Oh shit, looks like somebody forgot something. I bet she got pictures of this mysterious Fonz character all over her phone. I don't know why she be hiding him. He probably some type of weirdo or something." Shaky knew she had no business searching through Chameleon's phone, but she was eager to see the man responsible for having her best friend's nose wide open. Shaky began looking, and within seconds her mouth fell open. There it was, the recorded video of Geronimo trying to eat Chameleon's pussy while she was sleep on the couch. Shaky just stood there speechless watching it from beginning to end. Her heart broke into pieces as she fought back the tears that were about to pour from her eyes. How could Geronimo disrespect her like this, Shaky couldn't believe it. Not only did he try to eat her best friend's pussy, but he did it in her house! Shaky respected the fact that Chameleon had stopped him but was upset that Chameleon would continue to allow her to mess around with Geronimo without letting her know about the disloyal shit he did. The tears finally broke through, and began to roll down her brown cheeks.

171

Shaky tossed the phone, sat on the couch, and started crying her poor little heart out. Suddenly, she heard the door knob twist before it opened. She looked up with a face full of tears and saw Geronimo walk through the front door with a smile on his face. "What's up.." before he could finish his sentence, Shaky stood up and began screaming. "Get the fuck out of my house!" Geronimo's smile turned into a puzzled and shocked look. He stopped dead in his tracks, leaving the front door halfway open. "What's wrong? Why you tripping?", he asked as Shaky walked up to him. "Your trifling ass trying to eat my best friend pussy. That's what's wrong!", she barked looked him in his face. "Awe man, she done found out", Geronimo thought trying to keep his composure as his heart rate increased. Shaky saw that he was about to say something, and quickly cut him off. "Don't even waste your time and try to lie because I saw the shit with my own eyes on the phone." Geronimo was speechless, he glanced at the couch and saw Chameleon's cell phone. A dumbfounded look slowly crept across his face, all he could do is sigh and stand there. He didn't know how to go about the situation. "What you just standing there for. Get the fuck out!", she yelled before snatching the door knob and opening the front door even wider. "Man, it ain't even how it seem",Geronimo still tried to explain. "I don't want to hear that shit", she stated making sure Geronimo left the house. She slammed the door behind him and locked it.

Chameleon realized she slipped up and left her phone at Shaky's house, and went back to the house to get it. When she arrived, Shaky confronted her about the video of her and Geronimo. She wanted to know why she never let her know that he tried to come on to her. Shaky also told her that Geronimo just left and that she kicked him to the curb. Although Chameleon was surprised and a little upset that Shaky would search through her phone, she still maintained her cool and lied through her teeth. "I didn't tell you right away because I knew you was really feeling Geronimo and didn't want to hurt you or destroy your happiness." Shaky went for the bullshit, allowing the issue to rest.

CHAPTER 34: ATLANTIC CITY

Lunch had just been served. Gusto and Redrum, along with the other inmates, sat at the metal tables scattered throughout the day space eating and talking with each other. "Damn man. I can't wait to get the hell out of this shit hole", Gusto stated eagerly. Redrum sat across from him eating corn. "I bet you can't", Redrum stated sounding happy for his celly. "What's the first thing you going to do when you get out of here?" After Gusto found out Geronimo couldn't come up with the rest of the money, he took Redrum's advice and contacted the bail bonds from Atlantic City. And just like Redrum said, they were willing to take on Gusto's bail with the money he had. He gave Geronimo all the information necessary to make it happen. Geronimo was to meet up with Redrum's bottom bitch so she could show him how to get to the bail bond's, as well as be the second co-signer for Gusto. Gusto told himself that he was going to call Geronimo at 12:30 to make sure everything went through properly. "Oh you know what I'm going to do when I get out", Gusto stated smiling. "I'm going to find my old bitch and get all my fucking work and money back." "But what if she coming like she don't know what you talking about, or be on some cocky shit with ol' boy like she ain't giving you shit back?", Redrum asked. Gusto stopped eating his food and a devilish look appeared on his face. "Trust me, the way I'm going to come at her slime ball ass, she'll give that bread up. She ain't going to have no other choice." "Yeah, I feel you", Redrum stated knowing exactly where Gusto was getting at. Gusto noticed the dude from Redrum's city standing near the shower area looking at him chuckling. "A yo man, what the fuck is up with your peoples", he asked with a hint of annoyance in his tone. Redrum turned to follow where Gusto's eyes were fixed. The man immediately stopped laughing and looked the other way. "I don't know what's up with ol' boy. He

174

probably high or something." Redrum looked at the clock that hung over top of the C.O.'s desk. It read 12:32. "Ain't you supposed to be calling your peoples at twelve thirty?" That was Redrum's chance to change the subject. Gusto looked up at the clock and realized he was a few minutes late. "Oh shit, let me go hit this nigga up real quick and find out what's going on." Gusto dropped his spoon, got up from his seat, and made his way to the phones.

Gusto felt anxious when he picked up the phone to dial Geronimo's number. The phone rung twice before Geronimo picked up and accepted the call. "Hello." Geronimo was in his car driving down a busy street in Atlantic City. "What's good bro, everything taken care of?" "Nah, I'm in Atlantic City right now. I just got off the phone with ol' girl. I'm on my way to meet her at the laundromat right now." "Oh aight, you sure you know how to get to where you going?" Gusto asked. "Yeah, its right around the corner from the Tropicana", Geronimo's voice cracked. Loosing Shaky had him messed up in the head something serious, but the thought of Gusto finding out about his foolish act of betrayal had him shook all the way up. He even thought about just leaving him for dead in jail, but couldn't push himself to do it. Instead, Geronimo told himself he was just going to break down the truth about the whole situation to Gusto as soon as he came home, before someone else did. "Call in like an hour from now. Everything should be taken care of. I don't want the police to see me talking on the phone and pull me over on some shit." Geronimo hung up so he could focus back on the road as he drove down the long busy street. He made a left turn down a side street traveling in the opposite direction of the casino. Once Geronimo began surveying each street sign in search of his destination. Geronimo finally spotted it. "Oh shit, there it go right there", he said to himself happy that this shit was almost over. He waited for a red minivan to pass, before parking in front of the laundromat. There was a large group of people standing down the street. Geronimo noticed a dark skin female walking down the street in his direction. There were also two Spanish guys sitting directly across the street from him. Geronimo picked up his cell phone from his lap, and sent Redrum's girl a text message, letting her know he was parked at the spot. Within seconds, the red light on Geronimo's cell phone began to buzz, it was a text from her. The message read: COME INSIDE. HELP ME CARRY ONE OF THESE BAGS :) A grin appeared on Geronimo's face. After speaking to Rudrum's lady on the phone, and hearing her sexy voice, Geronimo couldn't wait to see how good she looked. He already had it in his mind that if she was a bad bitch he was going to push up on her. Geronimo put his cell phone down and was about to get out of the car, when all of a sudden his demeanor changed. His eyes grew wide when he looked up at the sawed off shotgun barrel pointed in his face. "Try some stupid shit and I'm gonna blow your fucking head off", the bare faced gunman stated in a menacing tone with his crazed eyes locked on a petrified Geronimo.

CHAPTER 35: THE TRUTH COMES TO LIGHT

Gusto paced back and forth in his cell like a panther in a cage. Redrum sat on his bunk quietly reading a Smooth magazine. "What the fuck is going on now", Gusto patience was growing thin. "Why ain't nobody picking up their phone?" He called Geronimo and the bail bonds several times, but never got an answer. He also had Redrum call his girl, but she didn't pick up either. This had Gusto's mind all over the place. Redrum shifted his eyes from the magazine to look up at Gusto. "I don't know man. I'll wait like ten more minutes before I call my girl again. Hopefully she pick up this time." Redrum's gesture didn't help calm Gusto's nerves at all. "I just don't understand it. The fucking bail bonds ain't picking up their phone either?" "They could be on they way up here so they could take pictures of you and have you sign your papers." "Man they usually make you come down to they office after you bail out and do all that shit", Gusto shot back. "Yeah, I know. But you from all the way across town, so they probably decided to do it the other way around", Redrum was still trying to make sense of the situation. Gusto stopped in his tracks and thought about it for a quick second. "Yeah man, you probably right." "You need to just calm down and have a seat. I'm sure everything going just how it's supposed to be", Redrum assured before looking back at the magazine.

Gusto just stood there staring at Redrum before he eventually sat down. "Yeah, maybe I'm a little too anxious." Without taking his eyes off the magazine Redrum grinned and said, "I bet you is." Gusto glanced down and noticed Redrum's legs rocking back and forth. "Shit it seem like you're just as nervous as I am. What you got to use the bathroom or something?" "Nah, I got bad nerves", Redrum responded. "You too young for that." Redrum chuckled, "I know right." Suddenly, the cell door swung open and a brown skin female correctional officer appeared in the doorway. "Mr. Brown, pack your belongings", she stated in a soft tone. Redrum dropped the magazine on the floor and stood up with a puzzled look on his face. "Where I'm going?" "Hell if I know. They just called down here and told me to tell you to pack up your things." The female officer turned around and went back to her desk. Redrum turned to look at Gusto, who was sitting there with a puzzled look on his face. "This must be A.C. coming to pick me up to go to court. I got a open case out there too." Redrum grabbed his sheets, pillows, and the rest of his belongings from his bed area. "You got my peoples number so call me when you get home", Redrum stated without even looking at Gusto as he rushed out of the cell. Gusto stood up and stepped between the door way and watched Redrum leave out of the unit with the escort officer. An awkward feeling came over Gusto as he began scrutinizing how coincidental everything was. "Something ain't right. I'm about to call Geronimo again", he thought to himself. While strolling down the hallway leading to the phones, something told Gusto to look across the day space. That's when he noticed the same man from Redrum's city staring directly at him, laughing. "What the fuck is up with this clown ass nigga", he thought to himself. Gusto reached the phones and began dialing Geronimo's number.

Geronimo was engulfed in complete darkness and cramped up in the trunk of his own car, struggling to remove the thick rope that was tightly wrapped around his hands and wrists. It was all a set up orchestrated by Redrum and his bottom bitch. The two young Spanish men that were sitting on the porch were the ones that tied him up and threw him in the trunk. The money they stole from Geronimo was used to post Redrum's bail. Geronimo felt his cell phone vibrating again in his back pocket. He knew the calls were coming from Gusto. He wished he could answer it and let him know the predicament he was in. "Fucking around with this nigga Gusto I got robbed for my last couple of thousand. I knew something wasn't right about this monkey in the middle bullshit", he thought to himself. His frustration grew as he continued to try and break loose. Suddenly, he remembered that he had his secret weapon on him. "Oh shit, I forgot all about my mu'fucking pocket knife", he exclaimed in between deep breaths feeling some relief. Geronimo slowly moved his tied hands near the side of his waist, and removed the small pocket knife from his belt buckle, carefully flicking the blade open. The cell phone started vibrating again. "Damn, I know that's Gusto again. Let me hurry up and cut myself loose and let this stupid ass nigga know what happened." Geronimo began cutting the rope with the blade, causing it to pop almost instantly. He pulled out his cell phone to answer before the last ring. "Why the fuck you wasn't picking up your phone? Where you at?", Gusto barked through the phone hoping his gut feeling about being set up was incorrect. "Because I got robbed, tied up, and thrown in the fucking trunk!",Geronimo was just as mad as Gusto. "Whoever put that shit together for you set you the fuck up. Now I don't have a nickel and you stuck where you at!" Gusto closed his eyes and took a deep breath. "Word up?", he stated feeling sad, shocked, and dumb. For whatever reason, he didn't want to accept the reality of Redrum befriending him, setting him up, and then bailing out with his money. "Hell yeah word up nigga. Matter fact, where the fuck nigga that put this shit together", Geronimo stated in a sarcastic tone. Gusto hung his head in complete shame. He didn't want to tell Geronimo something so humiliating, but he knew he had to. Before he could open his mouth to speak, Gusto took notice of the same man staring at him again, taunting him with his laughter. "This bitch ass nigga knew what was going on the whole time. That's why he always laughing and shit", Gusto thought to himself as he let go of the phone, leaving it hanging as he stood up and stormed back in to the dayspace.

179

With no hesitation, Gusto quickly walked up on the man and swung a sharp right hook that violently landed on the side of his jaw. The man dropped to the floor and was knocked out cold. In a rage, Gusto began brutally stomping the man out. All the inmates rushed to the wild scuffle shouting and cheering loudly. The two officers on duty called a code on their walkie talkies causing a swarm of officers to rush the unit. Gusto and the other man were escorted to lock up. Geronimo finally cut though the back seat, he was relieved to be out of the trunk.

It was 2:25 am, Fonz wore a black hoody and matching sweatpants. He sat in the driver's seat clutching a chrome 40 caliber handgun that rested in his lap. He was parked around the corner from Bo-Bo's house, getting himself together before he executed his plan. After Chameleon sold the dope to Bo-Bo, Fonz would lurk around to study Bo-Bo's every move. Fonz discovered everything he needed to know to take Bo-Bo for everything he earned. And, since Chameleon just sold Bo-Bo her last fifty bricks, now was the time to put his plan in motion. "This bitch ass nigga should be pulling up any minute now", Fonz thought to himself while looking at the time which read 2:27 am. He learned that not only did Bo-Bo's dumb ass stash his money where he rested his head, but he also came home the same exact time every night. Fonz climbed out of his vehicle and made his way around the corner, holding tight to his gun as he tucked it in the front pocket of his hoody. Fonz walked up on the house, surveying it for any unexpected movement. It was a dark green and brown house that sat in the center of the block, with large hedges along the sidewalk. "I hope it ain't no fucking cats in these bushes", Fonz thought as he climbed in to hide.

Minutes later, bright head lights gleamed through the darkness. It was Bobo pulling up in front of the house in his grey Buick with twenty two inch rims. After parking the

180

car, Bobo got out and began making his way towards the porch. Suddenly, Fonz jumped out of the bushes with his gun aimed at Bobo's head. "Try some dumb shit and I'ma bust ya shit", he threatened. Bobo was caught by surprise, he stopped dead in his tracks and put his hands up in the air. Fonz used his free hand to snatch Bobo up by the collar, dragging him to the front door. "Hurry up and open the door", Fonz growled aggressively. "Please don't shoot!" Bobo hands were shaking as he pulled out his keys to open the door. Once inside, Fonz used his foot to slam the door shut. All the lights were off, so it was extremely dark. "Where the fuck the light switch at?" Fonz was squinting his eyes trying to see through the darkness. "It's right there by the door." "Turn it on." Bobo reached his hand out towards the wall and flicked the light switch on. The downstairs lit up instantly, revealing the expensive looking furniture set up in the living room. "You know what I'm here for. Where the hell is it?" "It's in the kitchen. Man please don't shoot", Bobo was still pleading for his life. Fonz dragged Bobo into the kitchen, where he ordered him to turn the kitchen lights on. "Aight nigga, hurry up and grab it!" Fonz released his grip from Bobo, but his gun was still aimed at his head. "Alright man please, just calm down." Bobo walked over to the refrigerator with his hands still lifted in the air. Fonz watched as his victim struggled to move the refrigerator from its normal position, where he finally revealed a hidden door in the floor. Bobo opened the door, and pulled out a huge safe. "Hurry up and open it!", Fonz removed the black book bag he'd been carrying, and threw it on the floor beside Bobo. "Put everything in the bag!" Bobo unlocked the safe, and began stuffing the wads of cash wrapped up in rubber bands inside the bag. Once the safe was empty, the bag looked as if it was about to burst open. "Give it to me!", Fonz demanded. Bobo stood up, Fonz pointed his gun at him and stared deep into Bobo's eyes. Bobo gave up the money, praying that the stick up kid

181

would just hurry up and leave without harming him. Fonz aimed the pistol towards Bobo's legs. BLOW! BLOW! "Agghh!" Bobo yelled in agony as both of the hot slugs pierced his knee caps. Blood began to pour out all over the place. "Agghh!", he yelled again as he put both of his hands over the bloody wounds in an attempt to slow down the bleeding. He felt like he was starting to loose consciousness. The last thing he saw was Fonz running out the front door, then everything went black.

CHAPTER 36: JAILIN'

Several months had passed and Gusto was still having to go back and forth to court, prolonging his situation in hopes that a miracle would make everything better, but unfortunately it didn't. The justice system had him by the balls with hardcore evidence for a crime he really didn't commit. Gusto had no choice but to cop out to the only plea the court offered him, to serve 85% of a 14 year sentence. A few weeks after being sentenced he was sent to CRAF, a housing unit in which all the prisoners in the state of New Jersey were held temporarily until they were classified. Gusto saw classification his third week in CRAF, and was sent to Albert C. Wagner Youth Correctional Facility, also known as the Bordentown Gladiator School.

Dressed in a tan khaki uniform, Gusto sat in the back of the extremely long blue bus looking out the window. The driver carefully drove down the busy highway headed towards Bordentown, New Jersey. Every seat was filled with young prisoners who were talking loudly, causing the ride to be very noisy. "Damn man, I got to do twelve long years behind the wall for some shit I ain't even do. I'm twenty now, I won't be back out until I'm in my mid thirties", Gusto thought to himself. His sad eyes were still staring out the window, trying to catch a glimpse of the tall green trees and the forest like scenery. Gusto sighed deeply as he thought on his situation. He noticed a wavy haired light skin slim young man staring at him. "You aight?", Gusto asked wondering what the young man was looking at. "Yeah I'm good. I'm from Trenton", the young man replied. "Oh yea, you from the town? Me too." Gusto sensed that the young man already knew that. "Your name Gusto right?" Gusto shook his head yes, he really wasn't trying to meet any new friends, especially after experiencing what happened in the county jail with Redrum. But, since he said he was from the same city Gusto decided to give him the benefit of the doubt, knowing that in prison people from the same city had to stick together and hold each other down. "Where you from and what you go by?", Gusto asked. "My name Yellow and I'm from out West. I used to see and hear about you and your team out there all the time. Y'all out there winning." "This nigga sounding like a groupie", Gusto thought to himself. "Yeah we was doing our little one two thing out there. You said you from out West though, were exactly?" "Roger Gardens projects." "Oh so you know Bulldog and all them." "Yeah, I know all them niggas. The dude Young Bizzy got a baby by my sister Rayna." "Oh yeah, they still together?", Gusto was shocked but tried to conceal it. "Yeah, but I don't see what she see in that whack ass nigga. Don't get me wrong, he get bread too , but he soft and he ain't loyal to those that are loyal to him. He always kicking they back in to my sister." Yellow was venting out of frustration and resentment towards his sister's boyfriend. "Yeah, he ain't built like that", Gusto agreed as a plan began to slowly formulate in the back of his head. During the remainder of the ride, Gusto listened attentively as he picked Yellow's brain for all sorts of information. Once the bus arrived at the huge prison, Gusto and Yellow, along with the other prisoners, were escorted inside by a group of correctional officers. The prisoners were separated in to groups, and then sent to their assigned units. Coincidentally, Gusto and Yellow were sent to the same unit.

Gusto was fortunate to receive a single cell to himself. Once he was settled in, he tried to make contact with the outside but no one ever answered. This had him sick to his soul. To him it seemed like once he got sentenced, Geronimo disappeared and doing a bid without any outside support was one of the worst ways to do time. Therefore, he just stayed in his cell and laid in his bunk without going outside to the yard for rec. He didn't even care to see if he knew any of the other prisoners on his unit. The only time he left his cell was to get in the shower and to go to the mess hall. That's when he would occasionally see the young kid Yellow, and the two would have small talk with one another.

Gusto was laying in his small bunk wrapped in his white sheets dozing off, when he heard someone tapping on his cell door. He jumped up, opening his lazy eyes and removing the sheets. It was Yellow looking through the rectangular window in the cell door. "I could come in?", Yellow asked smiling. "What the hell this little nigga want", Gusto thought to himself. He nodded his head in approval, sitting up on the edge of the bed, placing his bare feet on the floor. When Yellow walked in, he sat down on the stool near the desk. Gusto noticed he had two big bowls of food in his hands. "What's good big bro, you aight? If you was in a deep sleep, I ain't mean to wake you. I just didn't want your food to get cold." Yellow reached his hand out to pass Gusto the huge bowl of food he made for him. Gusto looked at it and said, "Nah bro, I'm good." Gusto was hungry as hell, but his pride caused him to deny the meal. "Come on. You ain't been to the store since we got here, and I know damn well that shit they serving us ain't enough to fill you up. I be starving after I eat that shit, and I'm smaller than you", Yellow stated respectfully. "Stop acting like that and get full." Gusto just stared at him for a few seconds before he swallowed his pride and grabbed the bowl of food. "What is it?", he asked as he grabbed his white plastic spoon. "It's soup, rice, cheese, tuna, turkey sausage, and some special sauce I put together", Yellow explained watching Gusto scarf down his food. Yellow then grabbed his spoon and began getting his grub on. After taking a few spoon fulls, Gusto looked up at Yellow and said, "Damn this banging! You learned how to cook like this that fast?" "Nah, I ain't put this shit together by myself, a few dudes from our city helped me", Yellow admitted. "Oh yeah, where they at?" "They all in the day space eating. They all know who you is. They just don't know how to take you cause you always in

185

your cell. And when you do come out, you be looking like you ain't beat." "Nah it ain't nothing like that, I'm just going through a whole lot right now." Gusto thought about whether or not he should share some of the things he was going through with Yellow. "Yeah, I kind of figured that by the way you been playing your cell." Gusto, was feeling a bit insecure, and didn't want Yellow to think that he was some type of fraud, so he decided to speak on his situation. "I just been having a streak of bad luck lately. First, one of my little niggas got killed, then I got robbed of a few hundred bricks of dope, then when I go to see my connect to re-up they end of setting me up on some crazy shit, and after all that I get charged for murdering a fucking crackhead. And I ain't even do the shit!" "It sound like you been through hell and back", Yellow stated. He was surprised that Gusto had been though so much. "I see why you was moving around like you was." "That ain't even it. I was fucked up in the county with no bread, and my right hand man was on the street trying to scrape up my bail money. The bail bonds we had wanted more money than what we could come up with." Yellow was still eating, never taking his eyes off of Gusto. "So my bunky, some slick ass nigga from Atlantic City, told me he had a hook up with a bail bonds from out his way and he would set it up. Long story short, this nigga had my peoples robbed, and then used the money to bail out, all before I found out what happened." Yellow's mouth was wide open, and an awkward silence filled the cell. "This little nigga probably think I'm a sucker. I should have kept my mouth shut", Gusto thought to himself. Gusto started again, "Once I found out, I grabbed this other nigga from A.C. and beat the dog shit out of him. But Redrum is who I really want, I can't wait for the day I see that nigga again."

Yellow was still trying to process all this new information. "Well big bro. I know we ain't co-d's or nothing, but as long as we in this prison, we in this shit together. What's mine is..." Before he could finish his sentence, a tall brown skin correctional officer opened the cell door holding a thick stack of mail in his hand. "Mr. Anderson, you have mail", he stated. Gusto immediately stood up to grab the three envelopes from the officer. As the officer turned to walk away, Gusto closed the cell door and walked back to his bunk. When he looked at the name on the first envelope, he was clueless as to who it was, but his eyes grew wide when he read the name on the second envelope. "Oh shit, this my little Spanish bitch." Gusto anxiously ripped open the envelope, and began reading his letter.

Dear Germaine, I miss you and I love you so much. I'm very sorry about what happened to you and Flocko. I'm sure you caught on by now. I overheard him talking on the phone to someone, and he said you got sentenced to 14 years. I waited a few weeks and then looked you up on the internet. That's how I got your information. Well baby I'm always on the move, and I'm not too much of a writer, so I want you to call my cell phone. Anytime after 6 is fine. Oh yeah, I put $200 in your account.

P.S. We moving and getting married when you come home. :)

After Gusto finished reading the letter, he looked at Yellow grinning from ear to ear. "She used to work at the spot I used to cop from." He placed the first letter on the bed, and moved on to the 2nd letter and began reading it.

Hey Gusto, I know you probably saying to yourself who the hell is this. LOL. My name is Zakia and I been had my eyes on you for a long time, but I never got the chance to get up with you. One of my old friends said she know you, and was going to introduce us, but it never happened. So when I saw you in the newspaper for sentencing, I took the initiative to get at you. I got your info from the internet. I know you got a nice length of time to do, but that shit ain't about nothing. I'm a rider. I put a picture inside the envelope so you can see what I look like. I also put fifty dollars in your account. Here is my cell number, call me whenever. And put me on the visiting list, I want to see your handsome face. I can't wait to hold you.

"Man check this shit out", Gusto said as he handed Yellow the letter. While Yellow looked over the letter, Gusto took a look at the picture Zakia sent. "Damn she bad as hell." Gusto examined every inch of the beautiful young lady in the picture. Zakia had very exotic facial features, a smooth light brown skin tone, with light brown eyes. Her dark shiny hair was done in a unique style, and the blue and white dress that wrapped around her curvaceous frame made her look magically delicious. After Yellow finished reading the letter, he looked up at Gusto and began chuckling in admiration. "Ol girl on some straight up groupie shit. It sound like you got one on the hook." "Yeah, I know. Wait until you see this mu'fucking picture." Gusto handed the picture to Yellow, his eyes grew wide. "Damn! It look like she suppose to be on tv or something." "True. I'm about to call her asap." He took another look at the envelope, trying to read her name. It read: ZAKIA MCFARLE. He had trouble trying to pronounce her last name, but knew it was foreign. Gusto finally got to the third letter, from his baby mother Talaya. In the letter she wished him well and she included a picture of their 18 month old son. Without showing any emotion or mentioning it to Yellow, Gusto cursed Talaya out silently to himself and quickly put the letter under his mattress and made a mental note to flush it down the toilet later on.

For a few minutes Gusto and Yellow conversed while finishing up their food. Once done, they both left out the cell. Gusto hopped on the phone and call Zakia, while Yellow jumped in to the shower. Gusto and Zakia talked on the phone for a hour straight about all kinds of shit before he explained the visiting process to her. He instructed her to visit him in two weeks on Saturday, and then they hung up. Gusto then called his Spanish girl from Patterson, and they kicked it for the remainder of Gusto's time to use the phone. She told him that she wasn't going to be able to come see him until she got her work schedule switched, all her work days fell on his visiting days.

CHAPTER 37: THE VISIT

The huge rectangular shaped visiting hall was jam packed. All the inmates along with their friends and family sat in the fold up chairs that were organized in 5 rows. Two white male correctional officers stood at opposite ends of the room, watching with hawk eyes in hopes to catch someone passing off illegal contraband. "Damn what the fuck they turned her around or something?", Gusto mumbled in frustration. He sat in a chair in the middle of the visiting hall in the midst of everyone. He had been waiting for his visit for at least 15 minutes now, and his mind began to wonder. He looked to see if his visitor was walking through the entrance door, but she wasn't. He noticed a young Spanish man sitting close by speaking with his mother. The sight of the two made him think of his own mother. "Man I did some bullshit", he thought to himself as the tragic incident replayed in the back of his mind. Mixed emotions began to surface, he had to shake it off, so he tried looking in the opposite direction where he saw Yellow visiting with his big sister. Yellow must have felt Gusto looking at him because he stopped talking and looked in his direction. A wide smile spread across Yellow's face, and he gave Gusto a head nod which caused his big sister to turn and see who grabbed her little brother's attention. She was a shapely red bone female with full pink lips, and black straight hair that stopped shoulder length. She wore tightly fitted blue jeans, and a short sleeve gray and white designer shirt. No one in the city of Trenton knew her, she was the good girl type that only hung around in the area she lived.

Gusto smirked and nodded his head back at Yellow. He then looked at his sister in a flirtatious manner and winked his eye, causing her to blush. "Hey baby, what's up with you?", a female voice stated in a very sexy tone. Slightly startled, Gusto quickly turned his head to see Zakia standing with her hand on her hip looking fly as hell. She eased up on him while he wasn't paying attention. "Oh shit. I ain't even see you", Gusto stated with raised eyebrows. He stood up from his seat and gave her a warm hug and then took a step back, looking at her from head to toe. Zakia's natural hair laid neatly on her shoulders. She wore a tightly fitted white v neck t-shirt that made her perky titties appear bigger than they really were. The tight black spandex pants complimented her well built thighs and legs. "You look better in person. I can't wait to get home to you", Gusto stated licking his lips. Zakia began giggling. "Boy you starting already. Look at you." The two gushed at each other a few seconds more. "So what's up with you", Zakia asked still smiling at Gusto. "I be doing the same shit everyday in here. Working out, reading books, and eating hook ups with a few dudes from my city. You know, jail shit", he explained in a humorous way talking with his hands. "But anyway, what's been up with you?" "Well honestly, I was getting frustrated as hell because it was taking so damn long for me to get called out here for my visit. I started thinking you had some other chick come up here to see you", she stated eagerly waiting to hear his response. Gusto threw his head back, and let out a loud laugh. "You shot out. Don't nobody be coming up here to see me." "I'm saying, I'm not trying to dictate who coming to see you all early in the game or nothing like that. I just don't want to end up bumping heads with nobody. I don't have time for the drama, and I know those bitches probably kicking the door down to come see you." Zakia squinted her eyes at Gusto, waiting to see how he was going to respond. Gusto was lost for words, he was taken back at how freely and boldly Zakia was speaking on their first visit. "So what you just going to stare at me? You don't have nothing to say?" "Oh nah. I'm saying though, the only one be coming up here once in a while is my little peoples from out of town." "Are y'all serious?" "Nah, she ain't my girl or nothing like that. She just my peoples", he lied as he glanced down at the floor. "Oh. Well I hope her ass playing for keeps, cause I am", Zakia thought to herself determined to knock her competition out the box. "I just hope I ain't got to come home to you and be getting harassed by some crazy ass babydad that's dangerously in love with you." Gusto was smiling but was being serious at the same time. Zakia laughed, "Boy, I ain't got no kids." "Me neither." Gusto and Zakia continued to joke, laugh, and have good conversation up until the time their visit was over.

CHAPTER 38: GUSTO COMES HOME

Gusto was able to finish eleven and a half years, eighty five percent of his 14 year sentence, as best he could. He spent his time reading books, working out, and planning how he was going to get rich and seek revenge on everyone that crossed him. He also talked to Zakia and Neena on the phone almost everyday. Both of them proved to be loyal and stayed down during his entire prison bid. The two women never bumped heads; Neena always had a hard time changing her work schedule, but made sure she kept money on his books and on the phone. Zakia, on the other hand, took things to another level. She came to see him every week without missing a beat. She sent him letters, cards, pictures, and accepted all of his phone calls. She also smuggled weed through visits for Gusto, who told her he needed something to ease his mind. Gusto and Yellow became real close during the time they spent behind bars. Gusto tried to get Yellow to plug him in with his sister, but Yellow told him not until he came home.

It was 8:00 am on May 19th , Gusto stood in the day space with a white net bag that held all of the belongings he collected over the years. Yellow made sure he was up to see his cellie off. "So how it feel bro?" Gusto rubbed his hands together with a grin on his face. "I feel ready." "So what's the first three things you gonna do when you get out?" "The first thing is to get my fucking nuts out the sand. After like a week though, I'm diving back into the game head first. I ain't got no time to waste. I'm thirty one." It was if Gusto rehearsed this plan in his head over and over again. He even managed to stack five thousand dollars by selling majority of the weed Zakia smuggled in, this would help him get on his feet. A look of disagreement crept across Yellow's face. "I ain't trying to tell you how to move or nothing like that, but don't you think that's a little too fast to be jumping back in the game. You just did eleven and a half

joints. You should at least wait a few months, get a thorough feel on how shit moving in your hood first."
"Man, I been in that neighborhood all my life. Shit don't change around there unless I change it", Gusto started to sound cocky. "Yeah but that gang shit in our town heavy now, and it got them young boys out there wilding. Busting heads wide open", Yellow warned. Yellow was absolutely right. Gangs had flooded the entire city of Trenton, recruiting all the young boys who were babies when Gusto and Yellow was home. The recruits were killing people left and right, like it was nothing. "Man I'm good. Trust me", Gusto couldn't get with how paranoid Yellow started to sound. "Most of them little niggas I used to send to the store and give a couple dollars to. They know who the big homie is." Suddenly, Gusto heard the Sally Port door opening. He looked to see the tall, brown skin male correctional officer designated as his escort, walk on to the unit. Gusto and Yellow stood up to give each other dap. "Aight lil bro, I'ma holla at you. Call me whenever, you got the number to Zakia house. "Be on point out there. I only got seven and a half months left, so you already know what it is", Yellow told him as he watched Gusto depart from the unit.

Gusto had Zakia pick him up on his first day home. He was still trying to be a player and lied to Neena telling her he was coming home a month later than his actual release date. This way he could put in some quality time with Zakia before he dipped off with Neena. Zakia was seated in the driver seat of her car, bobbing her head to the Lil Wayne song that bumped through her radio speakers. When she noticed Gusto walking through the parking lot she beeped the horn, getting his attention. Zakia got out the car to meet Gusto, who greeted her with a long and deep passionate kiss. Once the two realized they were still in the prison parking lot, they quickly got in the car and pulled off. The only stop on the way home was at the corner store, where Gusto picked up a few things.

CHAPTER 39: HARD TIME

Zakia pulled up and parked in front of the red brick two story apartment complex in the quiet suburban neighborhood of Hamilton, New Jersey. The streets were very clean, and you seldom saw groups of people hanging around. She glanced over at Gusto, who was drinking out of a clear bottle of flavored water and said, "You alright baby?" "Yeah I'm good." Zakia stopped her engine, grabbed her purse from the back seat, and they both got out of the car. Gusto's lustful eyes watched Zakia's big loose booty jiggle in her dark blue sweat pants, as he followed her into the building. "Damn that ass look soft as hell", he thought as his manhood slowly began to rise. He let the heavy metal entrance door close shut behind him and continued to follow Zakia down the long hallway. The walls were white, and the carpet was dark grey. Zakia finally stopped in front of a door that read: 19A, and walked inside without having to use a key to unlock the door. "You left your door unlocked?", Gusto was shocked. "Yeah. I always leave my door unlocked. This ain't the ghetto. Nobody is going to come in here and steal anything", she told him with a small grin on her face. "You ain't going to be having this door unlocked with me staying here. Fuck that!" "Alright. Whatever." Zakia turned to walk in to the living room. "What you mean whatever?", Gusto stated in an authoritative tone. Gusto rushed behind her and grabbed her by the arm, causing her to spin back around. Zakia giggled, trying not to give in too soon. "Babe, what the fuck..." Before she could get the rest of her words out, Gusto shoved his tongue down her throat and began kissing her. Zakia went with the flow, and their tongues danced around in each other's mouth.

Zakia began rubbing her hands all over Gusto's broad shoulders and back. "Mhmmm", she moaned in between kisses as her pussy began to gush. Gusto, who was already rock hard, gripped both of her luscious ass cheeks and scooped her up off the ground. Zakia wrapped her legs around his waist and her arms around his neck. The noises and groans made them sound like two wild beasts. Gusto carried her to the white couch, and laid her down ever so gently. "Gimmie that dick daddy", Zakia moaned while looking Gusto in the eyes with pure lust. Her legs spread wide open with Gusto in between them. Gusto ripped his shirt open, causing his buttons to pop. After seeing his smooth light brown skin and muscular frame, Zakia couldn't help but to reach out and caress each part of his body she could get her hands on. Gusto began taking off Zakia's sneakers and then her sweatpants. To his wonderment, she wasn't wearing any panties. He dropped down to his knees and began licking in between her thighs. Zakia felt her body tense up, and a loud moan escaped her lips as she slowly closed her eyes. It was like heaven, Zakia was lost in the moment and she didn't want it to stop. Just as she was about to reach her tipping point, Gusto stopped and stood over her, watching her body wiggle and squirm for more. Pussy throbbing, Zakia began begging. "Daddy you eat this pussy so good. You ready to give me that dick?" Her soft sweet tone and raunchy words turned Gusto on. All that time behind the wall and it was really over. He pulled the box of magnum condoms out of his pocket before dropping his pants. "What are you doing?" Zakia sucked her teeth. "I'm about to put this condom on." "But I want that dick raw", she pouted. Zakia tried to snatch the condom, but Gusto managed to move her hands away. "Relax. Safe sex is the best sex", he told her. "Calm down Zakia. Just calm down. He's going to hit this good pussy raw sooner or later", she thought to herself trying to regain her composure. Gusto finished sliding the plastic on his

196

nine inch erect penis, and lifted her legs up to her shoulders. He braced himself for the feeling of being inside of Zakia. "Ahhh", Gusto moaned as he began fucking Zakia like a crazed maniac.

CHAPTER 40: LONG TIME NO SEE

Prepared for Gusto's return, Zakia took several days off from work. The two were able to stay in the house for two weeks straight, having out of control sex all over the apartment without any interruptions. When it was finally time for Zakia to get back into the swing of her normal routine, Gusto was left home alone. "I'm getting sick and tired of just sitting up in this tight ass apartment on some washed up husband, house potato shit", Gusto thought to himself. Gusto was shirtless wearing grey sweatpants, sitting on the couch with a bag of potato chips sitting in his lap. The Jerry Springer show played on the 30 inch tv. He had been fighting this feeling for four days now, and the boredom really started to bother him. He was extremely eager to get back to his old hood and see what was up, even though a part of him knew it wasn't a good idea. "Damn man. What the fuck am I going to do with myself", he thought as he continued to stuff chips in his mouth. "Fuck it." Gusto dialed a yellow cab service. "Yellow Cab Service. May I help you?" "Yeah, I need a cab to 153 Grant street." "Yes sir, we will be there in 15 minutes", the man assured. Gusto hung up the phone and put it back on the charger, rushing to the bedroom to get dressed.

The cab finally pulled up outside and beeped the horn. Gusto rushed out of the apartment, jumped into the back seat of the cab. The driver was a heavy set middle aged Spanish man. "Drop me off on Sweets Avenue", Gusto stated as the cab took off. Once they arrived on the ave, Gusto felt his adrenaline begin to rush. "Four fifty", the driver turned to tell Gusto. Gusto pulled out a five dollar bill, handed it to the driver, and left out of the cab. "Damn it's hot as hell out here", Gusto stated as he began walking down the steep hill. The sun rays shone bright. As he strolled down the hill he observed the block and saw a few unfamiliar faces sitting on their porches and standing around. "It's a whole new set of people living around this mu'fucka huh", Gusto was surprised at the change. Once he made it near his old house, a grin appeared on his face when he saw a group of young girls playing double dutch further down the block. "Aight good, ain't nobody near this area or paying me no mind", he thought quickly looking over his shoulder trying not to look obvious before cutting through the side of the house where a few green garbage cans were. "I hope this shit still back here", he stated in a low tone. He quickly made his way to the backyard and bent down to make his way underneath the wooden porch. There was a small wall of red bricks connected to the foundation of the house. Gusto pulled loose a red brick out of the upper left corner and dug his hand in to the open space. "Oh shit, it's really still here", he thought surprisingly as he pulled out a small bag. There was a 38 revolver snub nose inside it. Gusto stashed it before he went down to do his bid. You can pretty much say this was his if all went wrong weapon. Gusto quickly made his way from underneath the porch. He took the gun out of the bag and began examining it, he noticed there was a little bit of rust on it. He checked if it was still loaded, and it was. "This will do for now. I'll be damn if I'm out here naked after all the dirt I did, fuck that." Gusto put his pistol in his front pocket, and exited the backyard.

The new generation of killers, drug dealers, and gangsters were warring and taking over the streets, destroying anything that had life, and Gusto refused to be any where in the city without a strap. After he made it back out to the street, Gusto noticed a couple of people looking at him strange. He just kept it moving, hoping that no one called the cops. Gusto walked pass an alleyway towards the corner of Martin Luther King Boulevard and Sweets Ave. As he approached the corner, Itty Bitty came strolling around the same corner with a ruff looking handicap male friend. Itty Bitty looked a lot older and skinnier, and the filthy clothes he and his friend had on looked like they both slept in a dumpster for a week. "Itty Bitty where the hell you rushing to?" Gusto gave a slight grin as Itty Bitty stopped dead in his tracks. "Oh shit", Itty Bitty exclaimed with wide eyes right before his mouth fell open. His heart rate increased at the thought of Gusto finding out he spent all those years behind bars for a crime that Itty Bitty committed. Itty Bitty quickly regained his composure, going off the chance that Gusto will never find out. "Damn Itty what's up. You act like you sad to see me or something", Gusto picked up on the vibe. "Oh nah man, it ain't like that. I see you got your weight up and everything", Itty Bitty stuttered as a fake smile appeared on his face, exposing his cruddy looking teeth. Itty Bitty looked at the handicapped man, who had his head down, and said, "You see your boy Chopo." "Chopo?", Gusto was confused and lost for words. Chopo looked unrecognizable and was ashamed at what he become. His skin was darker, and he was skinny as hell. "What's good big bro", Chopo greeted Gusto in a low tone. Little Petey's death, Gusto going to jail, and the fact that he was crippled put Chopo in a deep depression. He lost everything, and eventually began hitting that glass dick, rolling with fellow crackheads in the neighborhood like Itty Bitty. "You got something on you?", Itty Bitty got straight to the point. "Hell no I ain't got nothing. What I look stupid? I ain't been home a month yet, I got to see how shit moving first." "Oh. Well we about to go up the street to find some", Itty Bitty stated urgently. "Ya boy just pulled off, he said he'll be back around in a hour. Come on Chopo." The two brushed pass Gusto, speed walking to their destination. "I can't believe Chopo really out here smoking crack. Shit is crazy", Gusto thought to himself. As soon as Gusto made his way around the corner, he saw a small group of young boys, wearing white tees, standing in front of a corner store. "Look at these little ass niggas posted up on my mu'fucking corner. I wonder if they out here working for Geronimo", he thought. Gusto never heard from Geronimo during his incarceration, and it made him wonder how he was living. Geronimo's absence also caused Gusto to feel a bit of resentment.

Gusto continued to walk around his old way, when a white Toyota pulled up along side of him beeping. BEEP! BEEP! Gusto stopped in his tracks and looked at the familiar looking bald headed man in the driver seat of the vehicle. "Gusto! That's you?" "Yeah it's me. What's up." He couldn't put a name to the face, but he knew the man was not an enemy. Gusto made his way to the car. "Damn bro, you look good. When you get out of prison?", the man asked. "I been out for a nice little minute now." The man could tell Gusto didn't remember who he was. "You don't remember me do you. It's Tommy." A few cars starting driving around Tommy's car. "Let me get a twenty piece", Tommy stated. "Man I ain't doing nothing out here", Gusto stated as he looked down on the twenty dollar bill he was trying to hand him. "Awe man. I was hoping I could get something from you. I damn sure ain't copping nothing from them young boys, they be having some bullshit." It was time for Tommy to pull off.

Gusto stepped back on the sidewalk, and made his way towards the store where the young boys were standing. Once Gusto reached the store, one of the boys stepped in front of Gusto, blocking his path. "Who the fuck is you to be out here making a sale", the young kid stated aggressively, raising his voice. "Little nigga you better watch who the fuck you talking to. You know who the fuck I am?", Gusto shot back towering over the kid. Gusto looked at him and could tell he was at the most sixteen. "I don't give a fuck who you is old timer", the kid barked harshly showing no signs of fear. As the young boy reached for the chrome 9mm handgun that rest on his hip, Gusto quickly pulled out his rusty snub nose 38 revolver. The two were now standing face to face with their guns drawn, aiming at each other's head. A few onlookers across the street stopped and watched in fear. Suddenly, the young kid, who by this time got a real good look at Gusto's face, recognized exactly who he was. "Oh shit, this my dad", the young kid thought as he froze up. BOOM! It was too late, Gusto took advantage of the young kid's hesitation and quickly pulled the trigger. He had no idea he just shot his own 14 year old son directly in the forehead, causing brain matter to splatter every where. The boy's lifeless body fell to the ground instantly. Blood spilled on to the concrete as his dying nerves caused his body to shake violently. With his gun still in hand, Gusto turned and started running down the street as fast as he could. "Fuck!"

Get the highly anticipated
Cold World 2 dropping
Summer 2017.